MW01051905

Special thanks to Mia Rettler and Joel Zuidema, whose feedback and encouragement drove this book to publication.

Edited by Jan Levin and Grace Claus

Delilah,

Lottie died last night. My parents are calling it an accidental overdose. They didn't want me to invite you to the funeral, but I know how much she loved you, so I hope you'll at least come to town. She'll be buried in Riverstate Cemetery. I'll let you know more once you get here. You can stay at my place, unless you don't want to. I sent you an email, too, so get to a computer if you can.

-Kari V.

Delilah leaned against the pink tile counter of the diner, staring at the checkerboard floors and the walls that seemed to be the color of some rarely seen internal organ. The diner was not well designed. Its parts were scavenged, or bought wholesale, the only qualifying factor being their affordability. The neon "open" sign spoke to a town largely disinterested in the establishment. There was only one costumer there, a regular. She was a hoarse-voiced hunchback who always ordered a glass of lemonade, a Caesar salad, and mustard, sometimes bringing a cake home for dessert, often slipping butters and sugars down her dress or socks.

The door opened and Delilah snapped to attention at the sight of Wes. He came in often for free crackers and coffee, but still left a tip, and when she was free they'd chat the duration of his visit. She walked back to the kitchen, where the cook and dishwasher were playing poker, to grab a pot of coffee, a mug, and a few packets of crackers. She placed them before Wes, then twisted her arms to place the heels of her hands on the table, leaning into them, fingers gripping the edge.

"So," she said.

"So... oh! So, yeah, I read it," he laughed.

"And what'd you think?"

"I thought it was hilarious, of course."

"Delilah?" The cook called from the kitchen door.

"What?" She didn't turn to look at him, keeping her eyes locked with Wes's.

"Did you use the good coffee pot?"

"No, I used one of the normal ones," she said, this time looking over her shoulder at the cook.

"Do you know where the good one is?"

"I haven't seen it."

The cook huffed and let the door fall shut.

"You didn't give me the good coffee pot?" Wes asked.

"No, I grabbed the first one I saw. Sorry."

"I'm very offended."

"Oh, really?"

"I don't think you'll get my business anymore."

"Psh, fine, I have lots of tables. I make *bank* on tips at this place," she said, deadpan.

Delilah watched him more closely as he started to laugh. He had dark brown eyes, dark enough to look black in the lighting, and hair that was shorter on the sides, thick and brown, maybe a bit wavy. He had the leanly muscled body of a pop punk musician or starving artist, and the cheekbones to match. If he had wanted to, he could have pulled off the grunge aesthetic, or become a pretty decent-looking metalhead.

He stared at Delilah as she let out a laugh. She had dark grey-blue eyes, the color of gun barrels in the sunlight, and a halo of nearly platinum curls around her head, falling just past her shoulders when it was down, though it was now tied into a ponytail. Her face was round and sweet, but her body was sharp and lean, looking unfinished, with plenty of angles and edges.

"So Wes, can I ask you a question?"

"You just did," said Wes.

Delilah glared at him in false resentment, then turned and started walking away.

"Wait, I'm sorry, it was ironic I swear!" Wes said.

Delilah stopped and turned, "That was unforgivable."

"I promise I will never say anything stupid ironically again."

"Okay fine," Delilah smiled and walked back to the table.

"So, your question?"

"Oh, yeah. If Josh comes in here again can I spill things on him?"

"Oh, please do. Like, everything. I don't care what you're doing, if you are carrying a liquid spill it on him," said Wes.

"Okay, good, because he was in here yesterday and I almost lit him on fire."

Delilah leaned away from the table to make sure her other customer didn't need anything. The woman was still working through her salad, which was covered in mustard and way more lemon slices than necessary, at least seven.

"So, did you get more medical?" Delilah asked.

"Oh, yeah. Still only ten dollars a gram."

"Do you want to come over and smoke tonight?"

"Yeah sure, when do you get off?"

"Around eight, if you want to come over around ten that'd work well."

"Sounds good," he said, "I can't wait."


Somewhere on the outskirts of Sedona, Arizona, an R.V. full of various cacti, houseplants, and visiting cats gave refuge to thirty-something Amelia Rackter. Loose, light clothes scattered the floor, and polaroids lined the walls.

But it wasn't the polaroids, or the cacti, or the cats that took precedence over her possessions. It was the ever present red dust that coated them. It wasn't that Amelia wasn't clean. It was just that the dust had a way of creeping through cracks, sticking to shoes and clothes and sweat, completely covering every surface that faced the wind and powdering everything that didn't.

It was here that Amelia escaped to as a teen, and it was here she had spent her adult life, living through online freelancing and writing.

Illness pervaded her body just as the red dust did, slowly enveloping her, caking on her skin, then falling into every other aspect of her life. The dust covered her sheets, and her clothes, trailed with her to the river and stuck to the inside of her lungs. She washed it off, but it was soon replaced. When she left town she found it still among her luggage. She left a trail of it behind her like a cat shedding fur. It was inescapable, ever present, changing in volume, but never completely washed away.

In Michigan it was the time of year when the trees had a hope of budding, and spring almost appeared, only to be discouraged by the return of snow. Still, if anyone could forget about the promise of spring for a few moments, the snow had its own beauty. Everything was wet and muted, but the air smelled like a thunderstorm and the subdued color scheme had a certain charm. Of course, it was harder to appreciate in the center of town, where the snow grew grey from passing cars and the water pooled in inconvenient places instead of sinking into the dirt.

Delilah's neighborhood had a distinct character, but its charm was harder to appreciate. The buildings sagged, the lawns were made of weeds, and the roads were littered with potholes. Despite this, Delilah would rather have spent the coming weeks here than in the brick and clapboard suburbs of her hometown, the last place she saw Lottie. It was the last place she'd been directly insulted or assaulted by her faux support circle who wore their beliefs like masks and laid them on others like shrouds.

She walked home from her waitressing job with her apron hanging over her arm, Kari's letter tucked neatly in her back pocket, along with the train ticket that accompanied it. The paper had grown soft with folding and refolding. This was the letter Delilah had carried with her since seven o'clock Tuesday morning, and it hadn't left her mind once.

It was also the letter Wes accidentally read in Delilah's trailer as she was pulling things out of her purse an hour later. Delilah's trailer was sound in structure, but that was its only positive attribute. It had a kitchen and bathroom, with a living room in-between. The walls were mostly wood paneled, the others covered in peeling wallpaper. The clothes she had were in a pile on a chair, next to her bed. She had a closet, but had lost her hangers. Wes didn't realize he shouldn't have read her letter until he had already done so. Delilah turned and noticed.

"Oh," she said. "That."

"Sorry, I didn't mean to read it."

"Don't worry about it," she pulled a few bills out of her purse as she addressed him. "So, what, seven dollars to get high with you?"

"More like five."

Wes knew all his dealers from his brother, who, despite being younger, got into drugs long before Wes. His brother had had hookups for everything, but Wes only ever touched pot. He pulled out a prescription pill bottle full of joints.


Ten minutes later they were sitting on stools next to the oven, blowing their smoke into the vent.

"So, what's up with you?" she asked.

"I don't know, not much."

"Well, how've you been lately? Last I heard Marie was still giving you shit over Adrian's brother's MIP."

"Well. I can deal with Marie, and Adrian's on my side, I had nothing to do with that. Still, I'm not sure how I'm feeling, you know," he said.

Wes was hurting at the moment. He spent a lot of time lying on the floor and sleeping. He couldn't hold a serious day job, which led to him committing some petty theft. Sometimes he felt okay. When he did, it was like driving along the edge of a snowstorm; sometimes the way suddenly cleared, but he knew that in a few moments he would once again be swallowed up in a haze he couldn't see beyond.

"I think I do, yeah." And she did.

"What about you?" he asked.

"... I'm not sure either." Delilah was doing alright at the time, but was left with a perpetual sense that she'd just finished crying; she'd feel a little bit good, a little bit sad, and a little bit empty. And she'd been crying a lot lately, especially when someone asked her how she was doing.

There were another few moments of silence. Delilah hit the joint.

"You probably don't want to talk about Lottie?" Wes asked.

"It's fine. I'll talk."

Lottie Druring's eyes had been black in the dark and golden in the sunlight. Her hair had been dishwater blonde, her skin porcelain with freckles and her lips more red at the edges. She hadn't smiled often, but she exhibited some internal form of joy. Delilah wondered if freckles faded away when someone died.

"I don't know what to say about her. We broke up just before I moved east, otherwise she might have come with me. Man, if she would have gotten out of that town I think she might still be alive, but how could I know?"

"So you're not believing 'accidental overdose.'"

"Please. Kari practically admitted it in her letter. Lottie killed herself, and you know what, I've heard people say suicide isn't as preventable as people think, and sure, maybe that's true. But if she just had someone to talk to who didn't either pity her or treat her like shit, someone who would actually get her the help she needed instead of telling her she should just decide to be happy or some equally ignorant bullshit, she would probably still be alive. If only someone from outside her idiot family would have helped her, you know. It's so fucked up."

"*So* fucked up," Wes agreed.

"Right? Anyway, she was an amazing person, she had many talents. Lottie's writing was very romantic. Do you want to see the letter she sent me to ask me out? It's very dramatic. Very *her.* I still have it," Delilah said.

"I'd love to see it," Wes said.

Delilah took a hit off the joint, passed it to Wes, and drifted over to a pile of small boxes by her cot, digging through them until she pulled out a worn letter in a fresh, white envelope. She walked back to Wes.

"Trade you," she said, smiling, and, after taking a drag, he passed her the joint for the letter.

It read:

> "You so often let on you want someone to love you deeply. You have no idea how easily I could slip into loving you. Every time I see you or talk to you I think, *this is someone special to me.* My memories are often tinged with my own charcoal touch but those with

you are tinted in rose and bordered in gold. You are, in many ways, the person I want to be and the person I want to be with. I admire you and yet I know the areas in which I am who *you* want to be, and that balance is what makes people really click, what really causes a reaction between them. The things we do together are painfully romantic for me, yet I know without a doubt I do not romanticize *you* because I also see your flaws and imperfections, get to know those areas where gold leaf chips away to German silver, and I don't mind that; I like silver better anyway.

All those nights we slept over and shared couches I stomped out my feelings for you. I didn't want to betray your trust, but now the fire has rebuilt and I'm head over heels, and I don't think I could tone it down if I tried. Maybe you're not totally straight, or maybe I'll be the exception to the rule.

So. If you're not straight, call me? Or send me a letter. I know you prefer it.

- Lottie Druring"

"Wow, you're right, what a romantic. Almost over the top, but not quite," Wes said.

"Yeah... she was that way about a lot of things... anyway. Do you want water or something?" Delilah asked.

"Do you have club soda, or ginger ale?" Wes asked.

"Nah, man. Just water and some diet cherry pop."

"I'll have water, then."

"Alright, cool. So, tell me a funny story Wes. I'm sure something interesting has happened to you recently." Delilah passed him the joint and walked to the sink.

"Oh, I don't know... wait! Okay," He took a hit and laughed. "Okay. Guess what I heard about your boss?"

"Greg? Come on, nothing happens to *Greg*."

"Not him, but his wife." Wes smiled at Delilah's realization of where this was going.

"Okay, that doesn't surprise me. What'd she do?"

"You know the cook's wife?"

"*No!* I mean, I know his wife, but... did they have sex? Please don't give me that image, Wes."

"Sorry, but yeah. Yeah, and Greg and the cook know and they don't even care," Wes said.

"That's awful. Ugh, I have this picture of two paper bags just..." she made some hand gestures, palms waving towards each other, "I'm imagining someone just slamming two paper bags against each other, like that's what that must have looked like."

"Whoa, calm down. That is unnecessary!"

They both laughed, and once the laughter started to die Delilah repeated the "paper bags having sex" gesture again and they started laughing again.

Within the next forty minutes, the weed kicked in and they started *really* talking, talking beyond gossip. Delilah told Wes about unsupervised campfires where edibles replaced s'mores and Wes told Delilah about his travels when he was younger. But in another half hour the conversation came back around to Lottie. Delilah was sprawled out on the floor, and Wes was sitting against a wall.

"I guess me and Lottie were just a high school couple. I don't even know if I should go out to Iowa. I mean, I loved her, but we've been over for so long. The only special thing was like, you know, everyone else thought we were super different, so we were like... it sort of just intensified this thing we had?" Delilah's voice was distant, her eyes bloodshot.

"I've never been in love," Wes looked away from the piece of wall he'd been staring at, back to Delilah.

"Did you love your family?"

"Some of them. My brother."

"I've never had a sibling," she said, pushing her hair back over her head.

"Hey, what time is it?"

Delilah looked to the microwave.

"Almost three."

"Do you have to work tomorrow?"

"Nah. You?"

"I'm out of a job at the moment."

Delilah stared at the ceiling and her mind wandered for a moment.

"By the way. I find your name very pretty," he said.

"Thanks. Ugh, Iowa. I don't want to go," she said.

"You don't have to."

"Yes I do... I don't want to go and face Kari. I mean she's okay, but, I've never had to deal with her *alone* before. I've only ever seen her with Lottie, 'cause they were roommates. They were also sisters but didn't really act like it. Anyway, it's easy to let things roll off your shoulders when you're with someone like Lottie."

Delilah cocked her head to the side with a sudden thought. "Hey, Wes. Wes... I'm just wondering, and, feel free to say no, but, do you want to come to Iowa with me?"

"Wait... really? Isn't there someone else you'd rather have go with you?"

"Well," Delilah started, "I'm not too close to anyone... anyway, most of them are from work. And none of them know much about me and I don't really care for them to find out like... more about me. You, however... don't seem to have a reason you can't go away for a week or so, and I don't care what you know about me, and you're pretty cool. So, if you want, I think you should come to Iowa with me."

Wes paused, looked down at his hands, over at the counter, and back to Delilah.

"How will I get there? You only have one ticket," Wes said.

"They can't be that expensive, I'll buy another one."

Wes would have asked why she would spend the money on him, but he felt like he was beginning to understand that behind all the eccentricity of her actions was a desperation for something, some feeling, or companion, or achievement. So he nodded.

"Alright, sure. If that's what you want. I'll come with you."

"Yay." She looked over at him and beamed.

"So," Wes said, bloodshot eyes crinkling at the edges, "what's the deal with paint anyways?"

They both laughed hysterically, and later fell asleep.

The next morning, the sun rose, just as one would predict. They woke up to the soft light filtering through the shades and the delicate scent of marijuana clinging to their hair and clothing. The two were sprawled out on the floor. Delilah slowly shifted into a sitting position.

"Still on for Iowa?" she asked, yawning.

"Uh, yeah, sure. Why not."

"Get here around eight on Friday then, and we can head to the train station together."

"I'll be here."

They sat without moving for a while, before Wes rose and left.

"Bye," Delilah called as he exited.

"See you Friday," he called back as he closed the door behind him.


Friday came, and Delilah spent her meager stash of emergency money on a second train ticket to Iowa. The sun was shining as it rarely does in the end of Michigan's winter, and the day held a fickle promise of spring's return as Delilah and Wes stood on the train station platform. The station employee who was sweeping the cobblestones didn't seem to notice them.

Delilah and Wes weren't thinking about the station employee. Delilah was thinking about Lottie and gay rights, and slowly getting worked up. Wes was thinking about trains. He'd been on one only once before, and remembered enjoying it. He felt they were fundamentally better than planes, because they connected people to their journey and the land within which they traveled across, not above it looking down. Wes believed strongly in avoiding that sort of disconnect with the earth.

Once the train came into sight, static started up in Delilah's mind as she realized she was really, actually, going home. Wes realized he was really, actually, going to to the home of a friend so she could grieve her ex. The wind created by the train as it pulled closer swept Delilah's hair into Wes's face, and she pulled it back towards her with her hand when the train slowed to a crawl, then stopped.

As the train snaked its way across the midwest, Delilah and Wes sat across from each other, both of them awkwardly wondering if this event was really something they should be sharing. Delilah slowly started to smile, and then laughed and Wes couldn't help but join in.

Delilah brought both hands to her face. "What are we doing?"

Wes laughed. "I don't know how this even happened."

"It happened because of drugs, Wes."

"That's probably true. 'Don't do drugs, kids, you'll end up on a train heading towards the conservative midwest.'"

"Or, '*do* drugs because you'll end up on an *adventure...* to *Iowa*,'" Delilah said.

"Ah, that makes it sound much better."

"It could be fun!"

"That is definitely not the right word," Wes said.

"Okay it's going to be depressing, but... there could be decent moments scattered throughout."

"Yeah, I'm sure. Okay, so tell me about where we're going. What are your memories from there." Wes leaned back into the blue plastic train seat in a futile attempt to become comfortable.

When Delilah thought back on her youth she remembered a lot of people telling her she was going to hell. But she also remembered towering oak trees being compromised by the cheap glow of multi-color Christmas lights as her younger cousins fished kittens out from under the couches. She remembered her breath hanging in the air as she sat outside a church at a December funeral waiting for Lottie. She remembered having to miss the burial afterwards because she had the stomach flu, and the way she watched from the passenger seat of an off roader as guests swarmed the hilltop like black flies. She remembered taking part in the weddings of her older cousins, dressed in various colors of silk and chiffon.

"Okay. Iowa," she said. "Well, there's a lot of corn. There's a small downtown with a bowling alley my friends and I used to go to. We went there after prom. Lottie and I went with two guys as our dates, and one other couple. There was a pizza buffet that really wasn't that great but everyone loved it because it was cheap. Lots of driving around for fun and running through parks and corn fields and also drugs, because I was with 'the wrong crowd.'" She paused, "How about you? You seem like a hooligan, you know, with the drugs and the sort of punk haircut. Were you a 'bad kid?'"

"No I was a literal boy scout all through high school." He rolled his eyes at his past self.

"That's cool. Now you know all about camping, right?"

"Well, I guess. I didn't have many friends, but I really wanted to be an eagle scout because I thought it would help me get into college."

"An eagle scout," Delilah raised her eyebrows, "Good for you."

"I didn't actually become one. I quit because I got fed up with some of the other boy scouts. I was technically a 'Star Scout', I guess."

"Why did you get fed up with the others?"

"Too country-club."

"Do you have something against the upper middle class?"

"No, it was just one country-club from my hometown that drove me nuts, mostly out of jealousy but also everyone there was entitled, very stereotypical. Besides, everyone in my town was just a wealthier, more conservative version of the people in the next town over. Like all the rich people got tired of their sub-par counterparts when the town was founded and all decided to move somewhere else."

"Maybe you projected your prejudice onto them."

"Maybe."

Silence settled as they both looked out the window at the passing trees. They filled the hours with restless naps and conversations about strangers. The train stopped a few more times, and on the second stop a young man sat next to Delilah, but he got off an hour later.

The fifth stop was for Delilah and Wes. Delilah kept an iron grip on her emotions, maintaining a straight face despite her growing panic.

Wes stood and brushed off his jacket. "This is our stop."

"I'm very aware." Delilah stood and followed him off the train.

Half an hour later found them standing at Kari's, and formerly Lottie's, doorstep. The white clapboard house was one of many lining the gently curving street, with cornfields stretching out behind them to abut a similar cul de sac a mile away. It was dark out, and the light of the street lamps caught on the humid air, creating a soft glow. Fireflies lit up in the rounded bushes and softly shook out their wings on the driveway. Delilah looked over her shoulder and saw the woman across the street watching through her kitchen window. Their eyes met for a moment before the woman snapped her lemon drapes shut. Delilah turned and stared at the mustard door turned brown by the darkness, with the silver knocker she'd observed many times before. The door swung open and Kari was inside, in an outfit purchased from some department store and standing on a rug knotted out of her father's old ties. Behind her an open home hosted generic abstract paintings in red and bronze, with vinyl couches and a granite countertop that was home to a small, but well-stocked, wine rack. The two women exchanged sad, quiet smiles.

"Hey, Kari, how're you doing?" Delilah asked.

"Well, not so great." She looked at Wes.

"Oh, this is my friend, Wes. I invited him along." Delilah just realized it might have been impolite to invite a stranger into somebody else's home, especially just after their sister died, but frankly, Kari had been so rude to Delilah for so many years that Delilah didn't care.

"Nice to meet you," he said.

"Pleasure," she said.

"So, it's getting chilly out here," Delilah hinted.

"Of course, come right in."

Kari headed to the kitchen as she offered her guests a variety of food and drinks. Delilah asked for red wine, Zinfandel, because she knew Kari carried it, and Wes took a coconut water, very pleased to find Kari had some.

There were a few minutes filled with the shuffle of fabric on vinyl as Delilah and Wes settled, the clanking of wine bottles and the sound of a cork landing on the counter, followed by the sound of wine being poured into a glass. Kari walked over with the drinks and everyone took a sip. Delilah looked down into the glass and drew the pad of her index finger along the rim, waiting for Kari to say something and feeling primarily fear over what that might be, or to what passive aggressive jabs it might lead. When Kari spoke Delilah tilted her head back in preparation for pitching an exhausted defense.

"I'm glad you came. I really am," Kari said.

"I had to. I did love her."

Kari was visibly trying to hide her discomfort.

"I know. I know it makes you uncomfortable, and I appreciate you still inviting me out, and letting me know. Really. Thank you, Kari," Delilah said.

"Well, I know you two were very close, it seemed right for you to come. Even though your relationship ended in a bit of a mess, you know."

"Not really. We had a pretty civil breakup, but I don't want to know what you mean."

"I'm just saying--" Delilah rolled her eyes as soon Kari said it, "--that you certainly weren't good for her."

"Can you not...."

"Delilah, I know you and Lottie were both Christians --"

"This again?"

"Delilah --"

"Kari, we've talked about it --"

"You haven't listened!" Kari snapped.

"Oh *I* haven't listened to your crappy unsupported opinion. At least I've researched my point of view --"

"It doesn't take a lot to understand the debated passages!" Kari's shrill voice, akin to a newborn, grated on the ears of her guests.

"You don't know the original language or context or *anything*. Now, if you actually looked at the evidence that supports your-- no, I'm not doing this again. Because I've had this conversation many, *many* times, I'm done with your opinions." Delilah narrowed her eyes at Kari.

Kari was about to speak, and Delilah cut her off. "Can't you see that you're *hurting* me?"

Kari was silent. Wes watched, not uncomfortable, eyes focused on Delilah's face. He saw a break not only in her composure, but even the edge that laid beneath it. There was a long pause.

"Okay, there are extra towels in the bathroom, the guest bed is made up, and I can put the futon down, so if you need anything else just let me know," said Kari, changing the subject, and then headed towards her room.

"Hold up," Wes said.

Kari turned and regarded him skeptically.

"...Where's the linen closet? I can handle the futon." Wes wanted to challenge Kari on her treatment of Delilah, but decided against it.

"Delilah knows where everything is, right?" Kari looked at Delilah.

Delilah nodded.

There was silence between all three before Kari left.

Delilah sighed. She rolled her eyes and pushed hair out of her face.

"I mean, really. Her sister just killed herself, just... she'll never let it lie. I'm willing to compromise my principles and just leave it. I'm willing to give up arguing if she would just *give me a break* once in awhile. I can't stand her, or this town, I'm done, so done with these *people....*" Delilah shoved her hair back, leaned from the edge of the couch back into the cushions.

"That must suck," Wes said.

Delilah looked at him and sighed. "Thanks."

"So, do you want the bedroom or futon?" Wes asked.

"Don't care. Do you want the bedroom?"

"I'm fine either way."

"You can have the bedroom."

Once Wes had gone to bed and Delilah spent a frustratingly long while lying on the futon, which, despite being clean and well kept was still uncomfortable, she headed back upstairs and over to the CD player in the living room. She knew Lottie gave Kari a few albums from "Collecting Matches," and that Kari didn't like them but kept them anyway. She opened a few drawers, looking for Kari's music, and finally found it on the bottom shelf of the book case. She squatted and shuffled through the CDs, enjoying the sound of them against each other, the comforting feeling of the solid cases through her fingers, and finally spotted familiar cover art.

Delilah walked back to the player and slid the CD in. She hadn't heard it in a while, and as soon as she did she became sad and uncomfortable with nostalgia, but she was too in love with the music to turn it off. Dress up box smell and peter the bear

"You still listen to them? I assumed that was a phase." Kari, apparently disturbed by the music, drifted into the room.

"I have always loved them, and always will love them." Delilah looked down at the cover of the album fondly.

"And I've always told you to turn the music down, and intend to do so again."

"Come on Kari, if you listened to them more I bet you'd find something in their music for you."

"I listened to them every second I was in the same house as Lottie," Kari smiled, "and never developed a taste for alternative rock."

"That's listening to someone else listen to them, not listening to them for yourself. I bet it'd be different if you really gave them a chance."

"I'm not saying anything against them, I just don't see what's so special."

"This was the first album I ever owned. And I haven't stopped listening to the music since." Delilah held it up.

"Well, I like the cover art. But seriously, can you turn that down?"

Delilah sighed, and her smile faded somewhat. "Yeah."

She stopped the music, took out the CD, and clicked it back into its case.

"Thanks," said Kari.

Kari left, and Delilah was left standing in the light of the one lamp left on, alone, staring at the CDs, missing a darker time in her life.

She wandered over to look at one of the squares of mass-produced art. She decided it was too mechanical. Too generic. It would fit into any home with too much ease. It wasn't provoking, it was effortless, a space filler. Delilah, having sufficiently judged Kari's general taste, returned to bed.

The next morning Wes and Delilah helped themselves to cereal and bananas while Kari held a small mirror in one hand and her eyeliner in the other, spreading brown gel along her lash line as she leaned against the counter. She retreated to her room for a few minutes, and when she came out she was holding a box about the size of a shoe box, wrapped in brown paper and tied with twine. There was a note scrawled on top.

Kari shrugged. "Lottie left this for you. Well, she left it for me with a note to get it to you. I wanted to deliver it in person. I would have done it last night, but you were tired, and, yeah, here you go." She set the package on the kitchen counter and slid it towards Delilah.

Delilah held it between her hands and looked at the note, which read:

"Please deliver to Amelia R, Morganson Lane, Sedona, AZ. Deliver in person. Do not open."

"I'm supposed to go to Arizona?" Delilah asked. "I can't afford that trip."

"Well, you could always hitchhike," said Wes.

"I mean, I could." Delilah looked at Kari, wondering if she'd offer help. She didn't. "Why does she want me to deliver it? She could have mailed it, or have me mail it."

"I guess you won't know until you get there," Kari said, and nothing more.

"Okay, I'll think about how to get there. I'm going to the cemetery. I can walk. Wes, you can come if you want."

Wes nodded, and followed Delilah as she headed out the door, not wanting to be left alone with Kari. The morning was bright, and warm. The leaves on the trees were just coming out, leaving a green haze among the houses, against green grass and new stalks of corn. The sun was bright, and the sky was large and pale. They walked silently for a block or so.

"So, what are you doing about Sedona?" Wes asked.

"Well, I'd hitchhike, but I'm worried about getting murdered or raped. I could see about taking a train or bus, but I literally have no spending money for this, especially not both ways."

Wes looked at her and grew concerned by her expression. Her brow was scrunched, she kept pulling her lips into her mouth, and her eyes flickered with anxiety. Over the next minute she started fidgeting, starting to grow more agitated, until she finally stopped and turned towards him just as they reached an intersection with corn on all sides.

"Come with me to Sedona," she said. "I'd feel safer if I weren't alone."

"Delilah...."

There was silence between them. She bit her lip in anticipation of his response, and he sighed. He didn't know how to accompany someone on a journey like this. He certainly didn't know who Delilah would be after long periods of time on the road.

"Hey, I really think you're a good person. I really like you. But I can't do that for you. I don't know how to travel cross-country for free. I'm not even part of this," Wes said.

"You know how to travel. And you know how to camp, and hike and things. You don't have a job. You don't have anywhere to be or anyone to stay with. I'm sorry, I don't mean to shit on your life, but really. Don't you want to go on an adventure with me?" she asked.

He sighed, and again, they watched each other.

"Wes. Come on."

"Delilah --"

"Please, Wes." She said it more softly than before.

"I really don't know about that. I don't think so."

She fell silent and looked down at the road as they started walking again. Wes did admire her. He did trust her, and he knew her well, but the amount of miles between them and Sedona intimidated him. However, he looked at her and saw her power and fear and didn't think she should be left to herself.

"Fine. I'll come to Sedona," he said.

"Wait, really?" she asked.

"Yeah. I'll hitchhike cross-country with you."

"Yay. It might be fun."

They continued walking until they got to a large stretch of pine trees on one side of the road, with gravestones that were organized in clear lines, but incongruous in shape and size.

"I don't actually know where she's buried," Delilah realized.

"We'll find her."

Delilah led Wes to the newest section of the cemetery and scanned for fresh graves. She walked towards a point where the gravestones lined a small creek, hoping the Drurings knew where Lottie would prefer to be buried. Sure enough, a freshly covered grave extended from a salmon-colored granite tombstone, thin, with roses etched along her name and date of birth. Lottie would have wanted something black, not salmon, with minimal design and a solid structure. But it didn't really matter, Delilah realized; Lottie would never come to lay flowers here.

"I should have brought something," said Delilah.

She stepped forward and looked at the grave silently. She didn't cry. Her love for Lottie, once blazing, was now no more than a soft glow.

"Maybe you should say something," said Wes.

"I don't know about that."

"I think it's what you're supposed to do," he said.

"So?"

"You might wish you had."

She shrugged, sighed and stepped forward. "Fine. Lottie, I loved you, and I sometimes wish you had come to Michigan with me. But really, when I think about it, we were just a high school couple, even though everyone else made it like more than it was. I guess we didn't have a future. But I really wish you had ended up somewhere that nourished you and cared for you. I wish you had found some other way out, even though I understand why you did it. I'll deliver the box you left for me. I'll have to hitchhike. That seems like the type of thing you would have liked and I can't afford anything else. I'm going with Wes. The three of us could have spent time together and enjoyed it. This is the last time I'm ever coming here, Lottie, but I will be thinking of you." Delilah reluctantly patted the gravestone and turned back towards Wes.

"That was nice," he said.

"It was a little anti-climatic," she said.

She stood and looked at the gravestone for a few moments, and Wes watched her.

"I guess we can head back to Kari's." Delilah turned and began to walk towards the road. They started back towards the suburbs. Wes walked over to Delilah's other side.

"What?" she asked.

"Your hair was blowing in my face."

"Oh, right."

"It's nice weather for a walk."

"Yeah, I used to bike on days like this, all afternoon, out to the dunes and back," Wes said.

"So you grew up in Michigan?"

"Yeah, Zeeland."

"I've been there a few times." Delilah imagined Wes as a child, biking through suburbs and then past country homes, out to the coast of Lake Michigan. She saw him leaving his bike at the end of the road, walking through the dunes, likely private property, and to the beach, sitting to watch the water alone.

He smiled before he said, "The woods and the lake were easily the best part of my childhood." -Same

"Me too, except I grew up with ponds and fields more than the woods and lakes. I used to leave the house early in the morning, just at dawn, especially in the winter. I would jog out to an old abandoned barn and sit inside. Sometimes I would smoke. I never really got a nicotine high though."

"I didn't smoke at all in high school."

"Yeah, I figured."


When they entered Kari's house it was quiet and dim. Delilah noticed Lottie's door was open at the end of the hall. Kari must have been in there that morning. Delilah walked over to it. She wondered if Lottie could have found someone else to room with, but maybe Kari was the best option anyway. Delilah shook her head as she looked at the door. Wes retreated downstairs, giving her time alone. She pushed the door open wider and walked in.

The walls were cornflower blue. Lottie's white bedspread laid on her twin-sized bed. The room was a bit small, and now that Lottie's things had been shuffled about, it seemed even smaller. There was a dress hanging over a box in the center of the room. Delilah wondered why it was out. Maybe it was one of the candidates for Lottie's burial outfit.

This plain white dress, long and light and almost see-through -- but not quite -- the one that billowed up around Lottie when she sat down. It had the power to bring Delilah nearly to collapse. It brought back forgotten memories, forgotten emotions. Long afternoons laying riverside, the glow that had occupied Delilah's chest when they were nearly touching. Hands brushing against each other in high-school hallways and the way Lottie's mouth pulled to the left when she smiled.

Delilah turned around, took a step out of the room, and closed the door behind her. Wes had moved into the living room.

He looked at her, and, not sure what he was supposed to do, simply asked, "Are you okay?"

"Yeah, let's play Scrabble or something."

At the end of her workday, Kari walked in on the two still playing the game, which had become heated.

"*It's not a word! These aren't words!*" Wes exclaimed with determination.

"Yes, it is! Kari! What do you call that thing people use to carry bricks?" Delilah asked.

"It's a 'hod.'" Kari set her keys and wallet into the little dish on her countertop, a dish designed just for this one purpose.

"And what do you call it when a cat is doing that spazzy thing and running around with it's eyes super dilated in the middle of the night?"

"'Woost'. Though, to be fair, I think that's only used by, like, three families, all of whom live in northwest Iowa. It's supposed to be Dutch, but I think we all know that's a lie." Kari pulled out a Greek yogurt and a spoon.

"Woost does *not* count," said Wes.

Delilah sighed. "Fine."

"Neither does 'smickle' if that comes up," Kari said.

"Smickle?" Wes asked.

"Yeah, like when someone's making cookie dough and you have a little smickle, or you smickle on it. Like eating just a little bit," Delilah explained.

"These words can only be used in really specific situations," said Wes.

"I'm so going to win this game," Delilah ignored him as she spelled out the word "quick."

"Have you figured out your Sedona trip?" Kari spun her spoon between two fingers for a second.

"Wes and I will be hitchhiking together," said Delilah.

"You have to start planning then. You'll need to figure out all your supplies, and what interstates to take, etcetera," Kari said.

"Is there any way we could borrow a few things?" Delilah asked.

"You're welcome to most of my stuff," Kari said.

Delilah looked at the couch, where the box sat. Wes followed her gaze.

"I *really* wanna know what's in that box," said Delilah. "How did Lottie even get to know someone in Arizona anyway? Kari, did Lottie go to Arizona at all?"

Kari shook her head. "Not as far as I know, but she did go on a few backpacking trips, about two weeks at a time, once almost three months, so it's possible she got down there."

"I mean, she couldn't have had a romantic relationship with this Amelia, could she?" Delilah started packing up the Scrabble game.

"I doubt it," Kari said, though Kari would doubt it no matter how compelling the evidence was.

"Wouldn't having one ex make a delivery to another ex seem sort of unlikely?" asked Wes.

Delilah sat staring at the couch, lost in thought. She finally got up and placed the game board back on a shelf.

"Guess we'll find out. Or I hope we will," she said.

"Call me once you know, would you?" Kari asked.

"Sure thing," said Delilah, not sure if she really intended to.

For the rest of the evening, Wes and Delilah looked over an atlas of Kari's, and began making lists of things they thought they should take with them on their trip.

"We should each keep a few water bottles on us," Wes said.

"Definitely. Plus some granola bars, maybe jerky. We might have to rely on the kindness of strangers for meals. But missing a few won't kill us," said Delilah, continuing to make a list.

"We need to bring a Swiss army knife, which I have."

"Sure."

"A map."

"Kari, can we have this map?" Delilah looked over her shoulder at Kari. Kari nodded.

"Okay, so we've got that," said Wes.

"Kari?" called Delilah.

"What?" she asked.

"Look over our list. Do you think we need anything else?"

"You could bring an umbrella," Kari said.

Delilah looked to Wes. "Do we really need an umbrella?"

"I don't know if it'd make that much of a difference anyway," he said.

"Okay, I think we're good on that. Thanks Kari. Anything else?"

"A towel, some baby wipes, deodorant -- but don't use it unless you can shower that day -- toothbrush and paste, some first aid stuff, toilet paper and a trowel, um, weatherproof sleeping bag... a tarp. Sunscreen. I have some old backpacking packs in the garage from Lottie's trips, so you could use those. I think that's it."

"Oh, yeah," said Wes. "That stuff would be great."

"Can we borrow some of the other stuff too? Besides the packs?" Delilah asked.

Kari sighed. "Yeah. Oh, and I'll give you my old phone. It's crappy, but it's still covered by my plan, so if you have an emergency you can call someone."

"Thank you, Kari," Delilah said.

"Yeah, thanks, Kari," Wes said.

"I think it's best we leave sooner rather than later. I'm not sure how long it will take to get this planned out, but we should be able to leave within a couple days, right?" asked Delilah.

"Sounds good."

They continued chatting and looking over maps for a while. Kari started dusting. Delilah couldn't discern why, but the way Kari picked up each little artifact from her shelf and swept a cloth over it a few times made her angry. Kari, with her little porcelain cats and pictures of family and her George W. Bush figurine. Kari, carefully inspecting everything because dust mattered somehow, books organized under some official system, countertops cleaned with vinegar, a different plastic container for every type of vegetable. That hanging fruit basket in her kitchen. That dish that only ever held her keys. A spare change jar shaped like a pop bottle, which would be dusted in a few minutes.

"Do you think we could leave tomorrow morning?" Delilah asked Wes.

He was taken aback, but still said, "If you want to we could probably get packed up tonight."

"I just think the sooner the better, you know? Kari, could you maybe drive us to Le Mars tomorrow?" asked Delilah.

"Sorry, I have to work early and it's in the other direction."

"Fine. I doubt we'll find a ride around here. I guess we can walk."

"That's quite a walk," Kari said skeptically.

"We'll be fine. Right Wes?" Delilah asked.

"Right-o."

"Great. We'll be great," Delilah said. "It'll be fun."


Amelia's leg rose slowly, hand resting on her ankle, arm outstretched as she lifted into her next pose. One bare foot pressed more firmly into red rock. She slipped out of the pose and cursed as she landed back on two feet. Sometimes she loved yoga, but today her emotions abandoned her and none of Sedona's wonderful mystics could make her feel better.

The sun was close to setting and it turned the sky and rock into perfect blues and oranges, complimenting each other wonderfully. Amelia sat on a fallen juniper tree and unhooked her crystal necklaces, her dreamcatcher earrings, her bracelet set with semi-precious stones, and let them fall to the ground. She sat alone in front of her trailer and stared into the west.

She had first met Lottie at a crystal shop downtown. Lottie was standing among the many bins of minerals, reading the placards that listed the healing benefits of each type. She already had a small bag full of different shapes and colors and as Amelia watched her she added a few more. One that was supposed to strengthen the heart chakra, another that aided sleep, another that eased the effects of depression. Amelia knew this type of person. They flocked to Sedona by the hundreds. People who didn't quite believe in alternative healing, but wanted to, *really* wanted to, to the point where they spent hundreds of dollars and endless hours investing in it. All to achieve some small measure of relief.

Amelia usually left these people alone, but Lottie caught her attention. That soft cataract of hair, long lean legs and hands with the same quality, long fingers caressing crystals and maple eyes flickering over the displays. She looked tired, in need of a shower, weighed down by a backpack and dusty clothes. So Amelia approached her.

"Hey," she said, "If you're looking for crystals, worry stones are great for beginners. It's less about the mysticism and more about using them as gentle reminders. If you don't have a lot of experience, it's good to have guidance from someone who knows what they're doing."

Lottie looked up, and her chapped lips pulled into a smile, eyes flickering down, then back up to Amelia's face.

"Really?"

"Yeah," said Amelia, "If you want, I can help you with the basics. I have a ton of crystals, you don't need to waste money here."

That's how Amelia got Lottie over to her place. Lottie was easily entranced by the dusty trailer and alternative clothes, the dozens of polaroids and the garden of succulents. She cooed at the cats and ran her fingers over the feathers of dreamcatchers.

"You came to Sedona at a good time, at least *I* think so. It's monsoon season, so there are plenty of storms," said Amelia.

"Well, I love the rain. Especially if there's thunder."

"And it's even better under these amazing Arizona skies."

Their first week together was spent cliff diving and hiking, trying on new clothes and sharing crystals, meditating at vortexes and practicing yoga. Lottie went home, but she came back a month later, and this pattern continued.

Amelia stared at the objects on the ground, reflecting golden sunlight, and gathered them up into her hands. At the trailer door she paused and sighed, leaning her weight into it. She knew she should love being here, it matched her personality perfectly. If she wasn't happy here, she should be able to find *somewhere* where she was. But now, even with handfuls of healing minerals in the light of America's most beautiful skies... her soul sank beneath her, away from her, into the cool dark earth.

In her trailer, she pulled out her flip phone and clicked through her contacts until she came to Lottie. She thought about different reasons to text her. Did she want any of her crystals back? Or her clothes? Was her sister treating her well? She took Amelia's favorite necklace, would she mail it back to Arizona? But Amelia flipped the phone shut and set it back on her bed. Lottie didn't want to hear from her anymore. That was fine. Most people felt that way about her these days.

Wes and Delilah set off around eight the next morning, packs on their backs, the box kept at the top of Delilah's pack.

"Le Mars is about a five-and-a-half hour walk, just so you know," Delilah said.

"Yeah, I don't mind walking."

Delilah smiled. "Good to hear. Because we'll be doing a lot of it."

Delilah spent a few moments processing her situation. She looked out and saw an empty road, and realized the amount of miles between Iowa and Sedona. She saw potential danger in the strangers they would have to depend on, and she saw the open land they may have to sleep in. And then she stopped smiling.

"Holy shit," she said, "I'm sort of scared for this."

"Me, too."

"Like, terrified."

"I know. I'm actually surprised you'd do this for her," Wes said.

"Well, who would I be if I just left and went home? I mean, what am I even supposed to do with myself at home?"

"What are we supposed to do on a five hour walk?" Wes asked.

"That's easy."

"Is it?"

"Of course. We have an infinite number of topics to talk about. So, Wes, tell me about your most rebellious high school experience."

"Yeah, that's not going to be interesting. You probably have much better stories."

"I'll go next. What did you do in high school that you weren't supposed to?"

"Well... once a friend and I decided to go camping. And we wanted to go to this one lake up north, but my mom thought there would be too many hunters there in the fall and she was worried we'd get shot. But we really wanted to go up north, okay? So we told my mom we were camping near the beach, when we really planned on going up north."

"So, did you go up north?"

"No, my dad saw us getting gas at this one station and knew it wasn't on the way to the campground we were supposedly going to, so we confessed and didn't go camping at all."

"Why didn't you just make something up? Like, you were going to get supplies for a campfire or something?"

"We were bad liars."

"You're right.That's a boring story."

"So Delilah, what about you?"

"Oh, I don't even know. There's so much. It was fun though. But it made me hate my town, and people in it," she said.

"Okay, so what made you hate it so much?" Wes asked.

"I guess... they all cared for me, and loved me, but... I guess I resented them for not realizing how much of my personality I was faking. They didn't realize I had problems, didn't realize what I was doing to myself. They didn't know who I was spending my time with, or what we did."

"What did you do?"

Delilah remembered plenty of things she wished she hadn't done, but there were some memories which were sharper than others. Memories that came uncalled into her mind. Right now, Delilah remembered when she was younger, mechanically drawing red lines across the skin of her hip, and wiping off the blood from the cuts and onto her hands and onto the safety pin. She washed the blood away with a cloth, and when she rinsed it, the water ran red. She ran a bath, and by the time she had gotten into it she was bleeding again, and chips of dried blood flecked from her skin, changing the color of the water. She panted for breath as her music played in the background, and when she got out she thought she would faint from staying so long it the water which was far too hot.

Then, later in the week, she sniffed her hair to appreciate the scent of cigarettes as she and her friends got high. Late that night she sat on a futon, dumbed, staring at the food channel and processing absolutely none of the tips for a perfect martini. At the moment she was calm, but when she woke up the next morning she was just as bad as ever, and the cycle repeated itself, again and again. By that summer her hips were lined with scars, other places of her body bearing small incisions, and her lungs had taken a beating from the smoke. But when people saw her at church in her dress with her hair up they thought she was just who they wanted her to be. She resented that.

"I self-harmed and did drugs and all of that," she said.

"Plenty of people went through that, you don't have to feel bad."

"Well, yeah. I still regret it," she said.

"Yeah... do you still relapse? With the self-harm, I mean."

She looked at him, surprised, but respectful of, his frankness.

"Well, I won't lie. There have been times when it feels like my whole life is a relapse, but not recently. I'm over a year clean now," she said.

"Good job."

"Thanks. Do you want a granola bar? They're really good, supposedly. Imitation maple flavor. That is literally what it says on the box. Not maple flavored. Not imitation maple. 'Imitation maple flavored,' Wes."

"I would love an imitation maple flavored granola bar, Delilah."

"Well, here you go. 'Kay, basic question here. If you had to eat only one thing for the rest of your life and health would not taken into consideration what would it be?"

"Am I allowed to eat one thing in different forms?" asked Wes.

"That's cheating, but sure."

"Then potatoes. You can have french fries, baked potatoes, mashed potatoes, double baked potatoes, potato skins, vodka. All great foods."

"'Foods.'" Delilah made air quotes around it.

"Okay, what about you?"

"Steak."

"Steak, potatoes, and vodka. We could have dinner together," said Wes.

"Who has vodka with steak and potatoes?"

"We do," he smiled at her and she shook her head.

"Okay, you come up with something to do or talk about," said Delilah.

"Hm, road games. Eye spy?" Wes asked.

"Okay, Wes, what does your eye spy?"

"I spy with my little eye a North American crop that yields kernels, set in rows on a cob."

"And that's it. There's nothing else to look at," Delilah joked.

The highway grew busier. Delilah held out her thumb but was ignored. They continued walking. A car passed and its owner glanced at them.

Delilah and Wes continued their walk. A pickup pulled off to the side of the road in front of them and the driver's head bent out the window.

"Where're you two headed?" the man asked.

He was an older man, with leathery skin and greying hair, but, oddly enough, especially considering his apparent fondness for chewing tobacco, his teeth were very well kept. Dazzling, even.

"Le Mars or Sioux City, if you're headed that way," Delilah said.

"I'm on my way to Sioux City. Hop in the bed."

"Thank you so much," Wes said.

The driver nodded, and leaned back inside his car. Wes climbed into the back of the truck and Delilah hopped in after him. They sat, facing each other. The truck started and they both slid before catching themselves.

"So, people are pretty cool, I guess." Delilah said, raising her voice so it could be heard over the wind.

"Sometimes they are, yeah."

"Oh, no, you're not one of those people who are always bitching about how much people suck, are you?" She tucked her hair back against the truck and pinned it there with her head.

He exhaled heavily in amusement. "No, no, I used to sort of be like that but... cynicism is a waste of time. It's boring and really sort of ignorant. I mean, I thought I was really smart for thinking everything sucks, but I've changed. 'Cause soon you realize you're not special, and after that I just felt stupid for ever thinking I was."

He used to believe people were lost, sometimes, in the demanding static that pervaded their lives and filled their minds. He would say their society was too often so repulsed by pain that they denied its existence, each individual so intently believing they must be the loudest that they refused to hear the voices of others. So focused on their own barbaric screeches into an unhearing void that they neglected to notice the world thriving and falling around them. That's what he thought, anyway. Before life actually hit him.

He'd become more optimistic, but held onto the basic idea. He still saw people as lost sometimes, but now he realized he, too, was a person. He found cynicism arrogant, boring, and even dangerous or parasitic, something that fed on its host and drained them of life.

Delilah nodded. "Yeah, me too."

Some of her hair slipped out and got caught in the wind, and she sighed. It was about forty minutes before they would arrive in Sioux City. The driver dropped them off somewhere near the Nebraska border. They thanked him and walked towards the neighboring state, close to a mile away. Delilah stopped at the sight of a dumpster and pulled out some cardboard.

"Stay here," she said to Wes, then walked into a restaurant.

"What? Delilah...." Wes peered after her in confusion.

She waited until the host stand was empty then slipped behind it, grabbed something, and came out with a sharpie.

"We should make a sign," she said.


It started to get dark as Wes and Delilah sat just between Iowa and Nebraska, Delilah holding up the cardboard and marker sign that read "Sedona, AZ" in thick black lettering. She pulled the box out of her duffle bag, and now it sat on her lap. They'd been there for a few hours, with no results. They could keep walking, but thought they were more likely to actually get a ride right there. One suburban looking family got out to take pictures with the state sign, but then drove off without a word.

"Wes, I don't think we're getting anywhere tonight."

"No, doesn't look like it."

Delilah looked around, then took Wes's hand and pulled him up.

"Come on." She led him to a nearby field.

"What are we doing?"

"We need to sleep somewhere," she said.

"Here? Is this legal?"

"This started because I wanted your weed," Delilah said.

"I mean... yeah, fine, you're right."

They walked to the middle of a field and laid down their tarp and sleeping bags. They laid down in the field, about a foot apart.

"I can't fall asleep like this," Wes said.

"Don't feel awkward, just pretend you're camping."

"It's weird."

"Weird is a social construct, Wes."

"Does that change the situation?"

"What, have you never slept in a field before?"

"Not like this," he said.

"Go to sleep," she laughed.

A few moments later she said, "Wes I can't fall asleep."

"Do you want me to sing you to sleep?"

"Would you?"

"Of course. Okay, what should I sing...*ooh* got it. Okay ready?" Wes asked.

"Yeah."

"Here goes. This is 'Flight of the Bumblebee, by a composer I can't remember," Wes said.

"Oh no."

"*Didleediddlie diddli diddlie doodadadaa doodada doo dada doo dada!!*"

"Please stop."

"Didleedidlili-"

"NO! I take it back! You can't sing me to sleep!" Delilah covered her ears.

"Is my voice that bad?"

"Shut up, you know what you did."

Wes smirked as Delilah giggled, and then they fell silent.

The field, which seemed drab and insignificant at their arrival, turned into something rich and velvety in the moonlight. The air was cooler, and so laden with humidity strands of fog began to form. Fireflies glinted in the corner of their eyes, their phosphorescence illuminating the chocolate of the grass just enough to paint it maple.

The night passed like all nights under the stars, part frustration and discomfort, part awe of the stars and the sounds of the night, and also a pride in acting on an adventurous spirit. They woke up every few hours, and were uncomfortable, but fell asleep again. They woke up before the sun rose and thought they were definitely up for the day, but fell asleep again.

In the early morning Delilah woke to Wes prodding her.

"Hey. It's morning."

"Oh. Good morning," she said, stretching into a sitting position.

The sun was just coming up, starting to push through the soft mists down onto the golden grass. Wes and Delilah quietly gathered their things and walked to the edge of the road. Delilah looked down the expanse of highway and grabbed Wes' arm, fingers digging into his skin with the intensity of her emotion.

"Wes, look, a *dog*!" Delilah carefully moved towards it, hunched over with her hand out, making soft noises at a sullen golden retriever who stood at the side of the highway, matted with dirt.

"Aw, Delilah! A dog!"

"Wes, gimme some food." Wes handed Delilah a piece of jerky.

"Come here, sweet baby, awe, come on, sweetheart." Delilah crouched and offered the dog the jerky.

The dog trotted forwards with the confidence of a dog raised well and grabbed the jerky. Delilah moved forwards, gently stroking its head.

"Aww, there you go, you poor, sweet thing. Aw, Wes, look at her. She looks so sad! At least I think it's a her."

Wes came up next to her and let the dog sniff his arm, "Oh this poor little thing. How can people let this happen to a *dog?*"

"I think we should call her Ruby. That seems like her name," said Delilah.

"Well, sure, but we can't travel with her."

"Oh, but Wes, we've at least got to take her to the next town so she has someone to take care of her! Look at her, she needs a vet." Delilah matched the dog's puppy eyes and pouted at Wes.

"If we can find anyone who will drive us with her."

"It will be easier getting a ride with a dog. No one can turn down a dog." Ruby began warming up to the two, and allowed Delilah to ruffle her dirty fur.

"I guess we'll find out." Wes sat down next to Ruby and scratched behind her ears.

"Aww, come here girl!" Delilah ran into the field and Ruby trotted after her.

Delilah giggled as she and Ruby chased each other, Delilah offering small gifts of food, and eventually getting Ruby to run after sticks. Wes watched her before giving in and running out to join her.

The morning sun turned the high grass gold, and caught softly on their hair and skin, lighting up their eyes from the inside, turning her dark blue to turquoise, and his deep brown to amber. Both came to a stop for a moment, laughing, and their brightened eyes met. Half of each face emitted a heavy glow, before Ruby came rocketing past and Delilah lunged to run her fingers over Ruby's fur. Delilah held up a granola bar and Ruby jumped up onto her hind legs for a moment to grab it.

"Oh, she's so trusting, I bet she has a family missing her right now." Delilah watched as the dog disappeared into the grass only to loop back to them.

"If we find a shelter we could see if she's chipped."

"I'd feel bad leaving her there though. She's too old to be easily adopted." Delilah lowered into the grass, hooked her arms around her legs and rested her chin on her knees.

Wes joined her, and eventually Ruby slowed down and laid next to them. All three smiled with the rare contentment of a warm spring morning, a soft breeze, a rising sun. A classic teal van, looking right out of the late sixties, pulled over to the side of the road and two women got out. Both had hair grown long, but tied up in buns, one brunette and the other ginger. They were covered in layers upon layers of tan lines, in athletic clothes and outdoorsy sandals. Both were lean and muscular, freckled, and at ease.

"Hey, what's up?" called the ginger.

"We're hitchhiking to Sedona. Can you give us a ride? We just found this dog," Delilah said.

"Aww, yeah of course," the brunette said. "I'm Eliza."

"And I'm Lily," added the ginger.

"We saw you guys and thought this would be the perfect place for a picnic, right?" Lily was grabbing a blanket and food from the back of the van.

"We found this adorable organic farm yesterday. The owners were so sweet. Oh my gosh, they gave us a bunch of extra produce, just because. We ended up spending, like, all day there." Eliza beamed.

"Yeah, the owner lady gave me this amazing recipe for quinoa salad. You guys are welcome to it. And all these fresh fruits and veggies, of course. I mean it's not breakfast food, but we don't really believe in breakfast food anyway, so... but here, we need to finish it before it goes bad." The two women were setting out the blanket and food, moving efficiently, like they were used to it.

Wes and Delilah joined them on the blanket, and held Ruby back from romping over all the food.

"So are you guys road tripping?" Wes asked.

"Oh, yeah, we have been for, I don't know, four months?"

"Yeah, like four and half," said Eliza.

"We're both travel writers and photographers, so we put these articles together and sell them to all these obscure little travel guides and magazines. We make enough to keep up our lifestyle," Lily said.

"We've become so close, we can finish each other's...." Eliza smiled in an overly cheesy way and looked to Lily.

Lily looked around in false confusion. "What? Why'd you stop in the middle of --"

"-- your sentence!" Eliza cut in.

Lily laughed. "You're such a little dork."

"Alright, who wants kale?"

They passed around kale, radishes, tomatoes, strawberries, apricots, and quinoa. The produce was colored brilliantly, with small bruises from travel, and almost overripe. The apricots left a mess of juice and pits and Eliza ate the hulls of her strawberries. There was plenty of kale left, but the radishes and cherry tomatoes started disappearing quickly. Eliza and Lily threw cherry tomatoes at each other and tried to catch them in their mouths. It didn't go well. Eventually both broke down laughing and shoved the tomatoes to the side. Eliza picked one up off the ground and popped it into her mouth.

"Eww, that was on the ground next to the side of the highway!" Lily said.

"So? it's a plant. It came from the ground anyway."

"Not nasty highway shoulder ground!"

"Psh, I'll be fine." Eliza smiled and Lily shook her head.

They finished the strawberries, and afterwards started loading up the van.

"Here, you can get in, but be careful of the plants," Lily said.

Delilah and Wes entered the back of the van, where window sills had been installed all along the inside, bungee cords keeping succulents and mosses in place. The seats were missing, a mattress lying in the back with a cooler and battery powered fans next to it. There were some minimal camping supplies set off to the side. They sat on the floor, Wes holding Ruby by his side.

"Eliza has this huge plant obsession," said Lily. "In case you couldn't tell."

"It's why I'm dating someone named Lily."

"Shut up." Lily pushed her playfully.

"I set all this up because I didn't want to spend so much time away from my plants as I travel. It's worked really well so far."

"How'd you get started with all this?" Delilah asked.

"I started buying plants and keeping them when I was, like, a junior in high school. And then I really loved them. They smelled fresh and they sort of just have this aura, and I stopped having bad dreams. If you hold one up against your chest and just sort of *reach out* to it, you can connect with them, like on a spiritual level -- Lily don't roll your eyes at me -- I know it sounds weird but seriously, have an open mind. These guys saved me in high school. You should try it."

"Just hold the plant and reach out to it, spiritually?" Wes asked.

"Yeah, try the moss closest to you, it has a strong aura."

Wes carefully rose to his knees and slid the moss from its bungee cord. He sat cross legged and leaned it into his chest.

"What am I supposed to be doing?" he asked.

"Just relax and breathe deeply, and then sort of push your energy out to meet the energy of the moss."

Wes shrugged and tried to locate his energy, breathing deeply and letting his shoulders relax, focusing on his heartbeat, but gave up.

"I sort of see what you mean," he lied, and returned the moss to its shelf.

"Yeah, as you can see I've just been collecting more and more as we move around. It sort of bothers Lily, but hey. So, you guys, tell me more about your thing."

"My high school girlfriend died and left me a box telling me to deliver it to Sedona with instructions not to open it."

"What?" Lily asked.

"I know, it's weird," Delilah said.

They pulled into the next rest stop to use the bathrooms and let the dog out. Delilah took charge of Ruby, hand resting on her head, as she took her over to the little park area. Eliza was checking on each of her plants, gently touching the soil to check if they needed water and brushing her hands over their leaves to make sure they remained undamaged.

"Her and those plants," Lily said. "She loves them more than me, I think."

"It's good to be passionate about something you can take care of," Delilah said.

"Yeah. Yeah, I'm glad she has them, she's gone through a lot of stuff, you know. She needs something like that. But at what point is it unhealthy?"

"When it starts negatively affecting her life or the life of others, I guess."

"Well, I can't say it's done that."

No one was around, and Delilah figured that Ruby had followed her everywhere else, so she sat back and allowed her to run a bit.

"Aww, sweet girl," Delilah crooned.

Wes came out and joined them.

"Do we really have to drop her off at the next town? Can't we just keep her?" he asked.

"I really wish we could."

Just then, Ruby, apparently spotting or hearing something the others couldn't, took off into the woods.

"Ruby, no! Come back!" Delilah took off after her, and Wes followed.

As soon as they reached the edge of the trees, they realized she'd disappeared down a slope, out of sight, into the woods.

"Come!" Wes shouted.

"Come back here, girl! Come on, sweetheart!"

They waited. Ruby didn't return. Delilah stood, mouth gaping. Wes was stunned. They waited longer. Ruby appeared to have left them.

"No...." Delilah groaned.

"Guess she's someone else's responsibility now," Lily said.

"What? No! We can't just leave her," Wes said.

"What else are we going to do?" Delilah asked.

Wes sighed, resigned. He shrugged, and they exchanged a defeated look.

"So..." Delilah said.

"Guess we're hitting the road," Wes said.

"I can't... I mean... damn, okay, let's go." Delilah led the way back to the van, where Eliza was finally content with the state of her plants, and was sitting happily.

"What happened to the dog?" she asked as the three returned.

"She ran off," Wes said.

"Ugh, no!"

"Yeah." Delilah said.

"Aww...." Eliza, considerably less content, huffed and leaned back into her seat. Lily got behind the wheel and took off, too fast, towards the highway. Suddenly Delilah, glancing out the side window through succulents, saw a streak of blonde fur racing into them just as the van hit thirty miles an hour.

"Oh, *fuck*, NO!" Delilah shot up and lunged forward.

Wes screamed. Eliza screamed. Lily shouted profanities and slammed on the brakes while swerving off to the side, without thinking twice. The van bounced up with a vulgar *thump,* then was propelled into a ditch, where it slammed into the ground forcefully enough for the delicately constructed shelves to come crashing down, one taking another out, snapping bungee cords, until all the clay pots shattered on the floor and into the bed and onto the camping equipment. There was a moment of absolute silence. Everyone was speckled with dirt, Wes and Delilah coated with it. Delilah had slammed into Wes, and they both leaned into the side of the van, fortunately unmarred by the shards of clay. Lily and Eliza were shaking in the front seats. The airbags of the crappy van had not deployed. On the pavement lay the golden retriever, body ripped open at one point, the edge of her ribs exposed and her intestines pulled from beneath them, splayed out along her length. One of her back legs twisted forward at an unnatural degree, and two of her paws were mangled stumps.

Everyone broke out in panic and sobs and screams.

"RUBY, *no,* Ruby, holy shit, no. Fuck, Wes, holy shit we just killed Ruby!"

"No, my plants, oh, my gosh, no, my poor plants! They're destroyed what will I do without you, oh, my gosh, Lily, are you okay?"

"IS EVERYONE OKAY?"

"The plants, do whatever you can for them!"

"NO ONE GIVES A FUCK ABOUT THE GODDAMN PLANTS RIGHT NOW. IS EVERYONE OKAY?"

"I'm fine."

"Yeah, yeah just bruises."

"Ruby is not okay."

"Goddammit, Delilah."

The four sat in a line on top of a picnic table. Lily rested her head in her hands.

"Do you guys have insurance?" asked Delilah, quivering slightly, trying to speak clearly over the vision of the crash pushed through her mind on a loop.

"No," Lily sighed.

"Maybe the van's okay," Eliza said, tears still running down her face.

"It is *not* okay," Lily said.

"I'm going to throw up," Delilah said.

Wes sat in a daze.

"Will we get in trouble for this? Like, did we break any laws?" Lily asked.

"I don't think so, but it's going to be pretty expensive," Wes said.

"We're all broke," Delilah pointed out.

"Well, we just can't get the van repaired, and we have the equipment we need to backpack, so... I guess we continue our journey on foot until I can get a hold of some help. Maybe my parents, or Isaac. So, Lily, guess we should pack up," Eliza said.

The two pairs exchanged numbers, waved goodbye, then headed in opposite ways along the highway, thumbs out.

"That was one of the most disturbing moments I have ever experienced," Delilah said.

"I have no words... dogs deserve better than that," Wes said.

"Also plants deserve better than that."

"True."

They walked in silence. The cars were back to ignoring them.

"Alright, well, I'm sure things will head in a more positive direction. They've got to," said Delilah.

"Where are we, even?" Wes asked.

"Umm...." Delilah looked around, waiting to spot a sign.

A few minutes later, she did. "Oh, come *on*. Sergeant Bluff. We've barely made progress at all. In fact, we're back in Iowa. All we did was move south like, less than half an hour."

"Hey, that's a half hour farther south, which is moving towards the southwest, where Sedona is."

"I'm not in the mood for your positive attitude right now."

"I'll try to get into a more negative mindset."

"Thanks. I just feel so awful, if I'd only have --"

"-- Delilah, stop right there. First, it's not anyone's fault, and second, there's no way to change the past. So, I mean, feel bad for a while obviously, but don't get caught up in 'if only.' Alright?"

"Yeah, thanks, Wes."

She reached over and held his hand. He accepted it without thought.

"This is friendship-based contact, just to be clear," she said.

"Yeah, I know."

"Isn't it sad that people can't just hold hands without everyone assuming they're a couple? Like, so much physical contact is sexualized," said Delilah.

"I know. Everything is turned into such a big deal. But also trivialized, you know?"

"Exactly. Right on." Delilah tried to wave down a car and was unsuccessful.

"Do you still have that sign?" Wes asked.

Delilah slung her pack off one shoulder to yank the sign out. "Yeah."

He took it and held it towards the highway, and after an hour or so, they decided to sit for a while. Delilah sat with her palms against the dirt, silently. Wes scooched in closer to her.

"What are you doing?" he asked.

"Praying."

"What for?"

"Not really for anything, more just chilling with God," she responded.

"How do you believe someone's actually with you?"

"Well, seeing is believing, right?"

He waited for her to expand on that, but she didn't.

"So... what do you mean? You've seen God?" he asked.

"I don't claim to have *physically, literally, seen* God. I mean, I've had experiences which are the equivalent of actual sight, if that makes sense. That's the thing Wes, I can't prove God exists, and I don't strive to, but I couldn't anyway because all my evidence is just personal experiences. I'd never just blindly believe something. I mean, I'm not stupid, I work at my beliefs." She made wide hand gestures and swept fingers through her hair as she became worked up, "I don't discount the creation story purely because I know evolution is real, I've looked back in history and read other's research to find why some stories are less accurate than others. If I just decided not to believe in it, I wouldn't be able to honestly believe the rest of scripture. It's the same thing with the gay stuff," said Delilah.

Again, they sat in silence.

"Of course," she continued, "the dumb, annoying people always seem to get the spotlight and make everyone else look shitty, and then everyone thinks we're all uninformed bigots. Whatever. I don't care about society's opinion of me."

"Yeah, I guess I've never been exposed to the more intelligent side of spirituality," said Wes.

"Have you ever believed in a higher power?"

"No."

"Well, maybe you should look into it sometime. Just to see."

"I don't know. The church has never appealed to me," Wes said.

"Don't even get me started on the church, there are so many-- okay, like the whole saving yourself for marriage thing is ridiculous. First off, it's a good way to have kids get married at nineteen, and it also creates an unhealthy attitude around sex." Her voice sped up as she continued, frustration keeping her words clear and harsh, "It's about following the course of a relationship and being honest about where you are. You can't just follow the will of your dick or vag, because it could be damaging to your spirit, but you can't just blindly abstain. People just need to be honest with themselves, and as long as they're not hurting or using anyone else, then whatever is right for them is what they should do. Like, for me, I had my heart and vagina sit down with each other and talk it out. And I ended up having sex with Lottie, and I felt good about it."

"That's very well put, and I agree completely."

"Yeah. So have you had sex?"

"Yeah. Yeah, sort of a lot, actually. Not all healthy sex, either. When my brother died – my brother killed himself, by the way – I sort of slipped into his lifestyle even though I *just* saw it destroy him. To my credit, I have only ever done weed, so I didn't follow in his footsteps with all the drugs, but I did sleep around a little bit, and go clubbing, I drank a bit more than I should have and felt like shit all the time. I'm better now. I think I learned a few lessons," Wes said.

Suddenly Wes' empathy over self-harm and suicide was explained, and Delilah trusted him just a bit more.

"I'm so sorry to hear that. And I'm glad you didn't do any hard drugs, because that shit can go downhill *fast*. Wow, suicide *sucks*."

"True."

The next half hour was spent in silent meditation, and then discussion of trivial thoughts, and then someone threw a wine bottle out of a car. It landed on a soft patch of dirt and was still half full so Delilah grabbed it and took it back to Wes.

The next hour was spent slowly sipping cheap wine, and then they got hungry and had trail mix and water.

"I guess we could start walking again," suggested Wes.

Delilah agreed and the next few hours were spent walking. It was interesting how their definition of boredom changed on their road trip. Maybe it was just that their minds were more prepared for it, or maybe it was the changing scenery, but they both found that empty hours on the road were far less boring than empty hours anywhere else. And before long, it was evening again.

A large car that looked expensive slowed down, and pulled to the side of the road. The driver stepped out, and the two simultaneously raised their eyebrows in admiration. She had a smirk rather than a smile, made by lips painted purple which stood out against her dark skin. Her eyes were almost black and framed with long lashes. Her hair was coiffed into a neat halo around her head, her body was soft and full figured, with sharp clothes that accented each curve. She looked between them, appearing to read them and decide they were likely harmless.

"What's up with you two?" she asked.

"Someone left me a box and we're hitchhiking to Sedona to deliver it," said Delilah.

"Anything illegal involved?"

"Not that we know of," Delilah responded.

"And you're from...."

"West Michigan, near the coast."

She looked between again for a few seconds.

"I can take you to North Platte as long as one of you drives for a while. I only got five hours of sleep last night," she said.

"Yeah, sure," Wes responded.

"Great, hop in. And don't try any shit, my dad makes me keep a switchblade on me when I travel and I've grown competent with it." She spit a piece of gum off to her side and slipped back into her car.

Wes looked at Delilah and they shrugged, then joined her.

"I'm Wes."

"Delilah."

"Nice to meet you. I'm Carmen. I'm going back home to Nebraska for grad school. Let me tell you, I'm glad for the change of scenery. I mean Iowa has great schools and everything but... Nebraska's more fun. For me anyway." She paused. "So what's up with this box?"

"My ex died and she left me a box with directions to deliver it to Sedona," said Delilah.

"That's... I mean no offense, but that's not a great thing to do to someone you loved, leave them a task like that with no explanation. Or, was there an explanation?"

"No, no explanation," Delilah said.

"I don't think that's okay, but whatever. Lot's of interesting experiences coming your way, I bet," said Carmen.

"I'm sure," said Delilah.

"So where are you coming from?"

"We got the box in northwest Iowa," she said.

"Oh, so you're just getting started."

"Yeah, we've got a while to go. Your help is really great," said Delilah.

"Don't worry about it. I think it's fun, and I would have had to stop at a hotel otherwise."

Carmen turned the radio on.

An hour or so later it got dark as Carmen slept in the back with Delilah driving and Wes in the passenger seat. Silence settled with the night, and everyone in the car receded into their own heads.

Delilah stared ahead at the highway. The headlights illuminated the terrain that gradually showed more curves, and long expanses of grass began to stretch out on either side. They entered a strip of highway far enough from civilization for the stars to appear, and the moon hovered high up in the sky, out of sight for Delilah. She glanced down at her hands on the steering wheel. Her fingers were too short, really, for her body, but they were thin and pale, and tipped with short, bitten nails. She looked back up. She tilted the rear view mirror for a moment to look at her eyes, and saw that they were clear and sharp, but two dark semicircles were forming beneath them. She stared out at the pavement. She hadn't been on the road for a long time. And never like this. Never this freely and uncertainly. And suddenly she realized, she'd made it. She didn't quite know how, but she'd made it out of something, out of some mold that kept her strapped between the suburbs and a trailer park. She was on the road now. She was driving fast, towards the west. And she felt, for the first time in an unreasonably long time; peace.

Carmen woke up after the third and fourth hour of the trip, and now Wes and Carmen were up front while Delilah laid out cold in the back seat. Carmen, looking less perfect but still stunning now that her makeup had shifted half an inch downward, looked back at her.

"Now *that* is something," Carmen said. "That's *exactly* the body and coloring I wished for as a high-schooler. That's the kind of girl my old boyfriend left me for."

"Well, I'm pretty sure Delilah thinks the same about you."

"Nah. No one fantasizes about my body before they see it. All this isn't supposed to look as hot as it does."

Wes didn't understand, but he didn't say anything. They were in hillier areas now, and could see bluffs and rivers.

"I've missed this place so much," Carmen sighed.

She directed Wes through the hills.

"It's gorgeous. What a great area," he said as the city came into sight.

"I know. Are you thinking of coming to my place, or do you want me to drop you off somewhere? My parents are in Switzerland so we've got the house to ourselves. Well, my little sister will be there, but she won't be much of a bother."

"Sure, it'd be nice to get a shower. That's very kind of you, thanks."

"It's my pleasure. Okay, turn left up ahead."

They ended up at the very edge of the city, at a neat log cabin, more expensive than the other houses in the area.

"You have a beautiful home," Wes stated.

"Yeah, I know. Here, come inside. "

"Delilah." Wes leaned around the seat. "Delilah, we're here, wake up."

Wes noticed her lips were closed as she slept, not breathing through her mouth like most people. Her hair was all over her face but it didn't bother her, so she must have been used to it. She looked so delicate like that, when her personality wasn't making up for her lack of physical mass. Thin limbs fell over each other, with a round sweet face like an old painting, not sharp and brutal like the faces of runway models.

She didn't wake up. Wes lightly shook her shoulder. "Delilah."

She snapped awake. "What? Where are we?"

"We're at Carmen's."

"Ahh." Delilah sat up and shook her hair back over her head.

"Come on, let's go in."

They got out of the car and headed to the doorstep where Carmen was punching in the code to unlock the door. She opened it into a tastefully decorated home, clearly styled and smelling of sandalwood. The colors were mostly whites and creams, with tree stumps as stools and furs as rugs, with wood floors and wide windows and accent walls tiled in granite. They saw an open living room with large windows and a fireplace, and a stairway on the side leading to a balcony that opened into the second floor.

"Gracie, you home?" Carmen called.

There was no response. Delilah wondered if Gracie would be up this late, but Carmen, apparently, had no doubts on the subject.

"GRACIE!" Carmen shouted.

"WHAT?" A voice came from somewhere above them.

"I'M HOME AND WE HAVE GUESTS."

"FINE."

"I'll show you to the guest room. Do you mind sharing?"

They looked at each other.

"No, it's fine," Delilah said.

The guest room was at the end of the hall on the upper floor, along with Carmen and Gracie's rooms. Wes went to shower first, and Delilah and Carmen sat on Carmen's bed.

"We should totally go out for drinks before you guys leave. We can do a whole night out thing, on me," Carmen offered.

"...What?"

"Drinks. With me, you, Wes. Come on," Carmen smiled.

"You don't know us."

"I like people. It would be fun. Besides, I'm very intuitive. I'd know if you guys sucked, you clearly don't, I can tell you're cool."

"I don't know...."

"Oh, come on. It will be good for you. When are you next going to have the opportunity to get pampered and dressed up?" Carmen asked.

"I don't have anything to wear anyway."

Carmen smiled deviously. She headed to her closet.

"No, come on. I'm not really a makeover type of person." Though actually, she was. "They won't fit anyway. I don't have boobs like you do."

"Certain dresses could work, I think. The stretchy ones maybe. I'm thinking this cute light blue dress or this slutty black sheath with waist cutouts, what do you think?" Carmen asked.

Delilah sighed. "Please. I'll wear the slutty one."

"Good choice."

Wes called from the hall to let Delilah know he was done with the shower, so the conversation was brought to a close.

"I'll probably wake up late tomorrow but tell Wes that you're both welcome to make yourself breakfast," Carmen said.

"Thanks. You're very generous."

"It's what I do."

Carmen's shower was stocked with body washes and cleansers and various high-end shampoos. Delilah hadn't used anything labeled as "luxury" since she moved away from Iowa. When she was finished, she smelled like mangoes and her hair was shiny and untangled. She had become relaxed, sinking into a good mood, and she thought, of all the people who could have picked them up, how lucky that they been found by this one generous, gorgeous woman. She slipped on a t-shirt and joggers and headed down the hall.

Delilah walked to the dimly lit guest room, which had an upscale bed and couch in it, all in tones of brown and ochre, with paintings of deer on the wall. Wes was in sweatpants, making up the couch.

"I got the bed last time, so I figure you can have it this time," he said.

"Sure. Carmen wants to take us out for drinks tomorrow. Also we're welcome to make ourselves breakfast."

"Sounds good."

Delilah slipped under the blankets and closed her eyes. She heard Wes rustling around for a while longer before the lights went out, and then she heard the sound of the couch sinking down a bit.

She woke up before Wes the next morning and headed down to see if she could find something for breakfast. She opened the fridge and mouthed a silent *what* at the full array of cold pressed juices, coconut water, and a plethora of leaf varieties, with very little in the realm of a full meal. Delilah pulled out the carton of egg whites and placed a pan on the slick black range.

Wes came downstairs, hair wildly ruffled, squinting at the light. He walked into the kitchen and leaned against the island, watching Delilah cook. She turned to look at him.

"Your hair is adorable like that," she laughed.

He reached up to ruffle it, "Thanks."

"Let me fix it," she said, leaving the eggs for a moment to walk over to him.

She carefully swept it into some form of order, then sighed, stood on her tiptoes and, starting at the back, managed to french braid it, leaving a stubby little braid resting on his forehead. She walked back to the stove. Wes peered at his reflection in the oven.

"Ah, very nice," he said.

"Yes, braids are the new man bun."

"What are you making?" he asked.

"I'm scrambling egg whites. I don't know how to do anything special with them, so if you want anything good you can make your own breakfast," she said.

"Did Carmen say anything about what we can have?"

"No, so I guess we can have anything."

He checked through the cabinets for food. After thorough hunting he found some organic wheat-free cereal.

"I've never seen a kitchen so oriented towards health trends my entire life," he said.

"Do you know what 'cold pressed juice' is?" Delilah asked.

"No."

Carmen came downstairs in a thin tan nightgown that stuck to her skin by the power of static.

"Carmen, what's cold pressed juice?" Wes asked.

"It's like other fruit and vegetable juices, but it's made by pressing the juice with tons of weight, and it extracts more from it. My mom orders them in bulk from this company her friend started. Want one?"

"Sure," Delilah said.

Carmen picked out a green juice for herself and handed Wes and Delilah red juices. "They're not that bad, I promise."

Delilah finished the eggs, so she grabbed a plate and shuffled them onto it, then took a sip of juice.

"It tastes like health," she said.

Wes tried it. "Yeah, I agree."

"So," Carmen said. "The plan for today. I was thinking a little tour of the town. Visit some shops. See some sights. End with some drinking, and call it a day?"

"That sounds like fun," said Wes.

"It's a plan," agreed Delilah.

"Wes, let me fix your hair," said Carmen.


Later that morning the three found themselves in an antique shop on their tour of the city. Delilah and Wes continuously nudged each other and nodded to different items. The toys were all grungy vintage, with missing eyes and cracked lips, the books sectioned off by their target races. There was an entire section of cards simply labeled "Indian Related," and another, arguably more offensive section labeled, "Jews." Delilah took in all the Confederate flag merchandise, the quantity of which was surprising, considering they weren't even in the South, and discreetly hid it in corners of the store. Wes collected all the clown toys into one basket, just for fun. While Delilah flipped through a housekeeping guide, Wes held a stuffed squirrel posed with a rifle and Confederate flag up to Delilah's shoulder. She jumped when she noticed it and Wes laughed.

"That's not a toy," the lady at the desk snapped.

"Oh, yeah, sorry." Wes put it down and he and Delilah giggled.

"You guys are having too much fun." Carmen rolled her eyes at them.

"Check out this old radio. The tag says it still works," Wes noticed.

"Man, I wish I could get that, that's sweet," Delilah said.

Carmen checked the tag. "Hey, it's only seventy bucks. I'm totally getting this for my room."

They left with the radio and decided they didn't need to tour any of the city's signature attractions. Carmen insisted on treating them to lunch, so they found a cute little cafe that Carmen claimed had good sandwiches and surprisingly impressive coffee.

The cafe was painted in warm tones, with local artists' work on the walls and soft gold lighting. The barista greeted Carmen as she walked in.

"David, these are my friends, Wes and Delilah. They're hitchhiking to Sedona," Carmen said.

"Hey, guys," David said.

"So, any wonderful new roasts?" Carmen asked.

"No, we only have the five. As usual."

"Darn."

"Yeah."

"I'll have a French roast coffee, cold brew please," Carmen ordered.

"I already have it ready for you. And you two?"

"A cappuccino," Wes said.

"I'll have a shot in the dark with an extra shot of espresso, please," said Delilah.

Carmen paid while Wes and Delilah found a booth. Carmen artfully managed to carry three drinks back to the table by herself.

"I don't believe in cappuccinos," Delilah said, watching Wes drink his.

"What?" he asked.

"They just -- I mean, they're just too close to lattes. They have more foam and that's it."

"But you do believe in them, like you know they exist," Wes said.

"I don't put stock in them though. I'm not willing to get behind them. I wouldn't bother ordering one or making one. I do believe cappuccinos exist. I don't *believe in* them." Delilah sipped her black coffee with three shots of espresso and watched Wes to see if he understood.

"I honestly don't care," said Carmen.

Feeling a little condescended to by her implication that their opinions were juvenile, they let Carmen lead the conversation from there on out.

Afterwards, Carmen insisted on taking them out to a movie, so they went. It was a rom-com, with two pretty people stumbling around New York City, falling in love in a matter of weeks, falling out of love over a miscommunication and then realizing they made a mistake and getting back together. There was a fair amount of eye rolling between the three of them, but they all secretly enjoyed it.

Carmen then insisted on taking Delilah to get acrylic nails. She said Wes should get his hair fixed up.

"You're spending too much money on us. We don't need this, honestly," Delilah protested.

"But you'll enjoy it, and, not to sound like a spoiled brat or anything, but it's my parent's money and they honestly have too much of it. Yeah, that sounded bratty. But seriously, acrylic nails are the shit. Come on Delilah. I'm going to make you get them." Carmen beamed sweetly, and Delilah agreed.

"Wes, you should get them too," Delilah said when they reached the nail parlor, but Wes declined, and hung around some nearby thrift shops instead.

"Have you gotten these before?" Carmen asked.

"No."

"You'll love them. They have different shapes. Last time I had them, I got 'almond.' It's like, almost pointy, but not like stilettos." She pointed at a picture on the wall. "Like that."

Carmen continued to guide Delilah through the rest of the process.

"No, don't get them any shorter. It will look weird once they're done," Carmen said when Delilah was asked if the length was okay, and when asked if the shape of a nail was to her standards Carmen said, "Tell him that one is uneven."

When the nails were almost finished Carmen advised Delilah to go for black polish. Delilah had them painted black, as Carmen suggested, but sort of wondered if she should have chosen grey, like the girl next to her.

On the way to get Wes' hair done, Delilah tapped her nails against any hard surface she could. At that moment, she tapped them against the window.

"*Delilah,*" Wes said, for a third time.

Delilah pulled an intense face as she stared Wes down, and slowly rose her hand to the window, deliberately clacked each nail against it.

"Nah I'm kidding. I'm done now, sorry," she said.

Wes rolled his eyes and laughed.

"You know Wes, if you let the top grow even longer and kept the sides short, you could do the whole man bun thing," Carmen suggested.

"Wes, please don't grow hair long enough for a bun on only the top of your head. Any side hair to top hair ratio more dramatic than what you have now is just ridiculous."

"I think buns are sort of hot," Carmen said. "I know the guy who runs this salon. He gives me a discount because we used to have sex."

Carmen's ex-lover, Javier, greeted them warmly upon their arrival, and tried to talk all three of them into a haircut. Carmen insisted on Wes only, who was sent to a chair to be worked on by someone who wasn't Javier. Carmen and Delilah surveyed the beauty products for sale in the entry way.

"Ever tried this? It's made completely from essential oils," Carmen said.

"No."

"It works wonders. What about this? It's tea tree oil. It balances the pH of your scalp."

"No."

"Delilah, please tell me you've at least tried *some* version of this stuff. Look, it has real pieces of lavender in it. True lavender, grown in the south of France."

"No."

"You're making me sad. What about this? It's a salt water spray for your skin and hair that makes it look better."

"I haven't seen any of this stuff before," Delilah said.

"You're missing out."

Delilah wondered what she could really be missing out on. What chunks of lavender, no matter their origin, could possibly contribute to her quality of life, but she didn't say anything.

Wes came back with his hair sharpened up half an hour later, and by then it was getting late enough to go out for drinks, so Carmen took Delilah back to her house to get ready. She took a designer shirt and strategically ripped skinny jeans from her brother's room.

"He took most of his stuff to college, and he's not exactly your size, but hey." She shoved them at Wes.

"I don't know about this," he said.

"Wear the skinny jeans," Carmen said.

Carmen changed into a bright white dress, with beading that made it sparkle at certain angles. Then she had Delilah change, and then started on her makeup, leaning in close enough for Delilah to smell spicy perfume and feel Carmen's breath as soft brushes and light fingers moved across her face. Delilah remembered Lottie doing this to her once. There had been giggles and kisses. She so clearly remembered Lottie telling her to open her eyes and Lottie staring into them, checking to make sure the eyeliner was symmetrical.

"Open your eyes... okay close them. Look up. Okay, part your lips a bit... suck your cheeks in for a second." Carmen rattled off instructions as she worked.

"And... open your eyes!" Carmen exclaimed.

Delilah opened her eyes and saw herself all in black, with dark makeup and her hair falling down her back.

"Wow, I don't know if I've ever looked anything like this before," she said.

"That's a shame. This is a good look for you."


Carmen took them to a dimly lit, smoky bar and ordered an Old Fashioned. As she leaned over the bar to reach for her drink, both Delilah and Wes were caught up in the way the light moved on her hair and shoulder blades. They both looked at her, then at each other and, in that moment, both knew where the other had been looking. Delilah's jaw unhinged slightly as Wes looked up at the ceiling and sighed. When Carmen turned around she was completely unaware of what had just passed between them.

"Do you guys want anything? I'll pay. Obviously."

"Um. No, I'm good." Wes smirked slightly at Delilah.

"Vodka tonic." Delilah's shifted her attention back to Carmen, smiling too sweetly.

Wes raised his eyebrows at her and smirked in an *ooh, someone has a crush* face, and she sneered back at him.

After hours of light chatter and heavy drinks, Wes was sober, Delilah was buzzed, and Carmen slouched against the bar, slurring sentences and waving her hands through the air as she spoke. Wes and Delilah had to help her walk out to the car. And another life disappointment began crystalizing before them.

Plenty of things aren't true. For example, looks *do* matter. Knock-offs don't look like the originals. "Lite" restaurant dishes still have too many calories for someone on a diet. Jeans don't go with everything. Not everyone can pull off candy apple red lipstick, no matter their level of confidence. And Carmen wasn't special.

As she was laying in the backseat of the car, covered in her own vomit, with her dress slipping and her makeup smudged to one side of her face, suddenly she was not the generous, gorgeous and perfect woman who appeared like an angel who whisked them into utopia. She was just another college student with a nice body and rich parents, who had found her way into a life of spontaneity that brought her out of real life whenever possible, be it with drugs, alcohol, or picking up strangers on the highway and doing their makeup and giving them coffee. The glass pedestal Delilah and Wes had unconsciously built beneath her shattered.

They got home and carried Carmen upstairs. Gracie glanced at them and let out a harsh laugh at Carmen's condition before retreating back into her room. Delilah thought Gracie shot her a dirty look, but couldn't be sure. Wes and Delilah, too tired to shower, stripped down to underwear and went to sleep, this time with Wes taking the bed.


The next morning Carmen invited them to stay another day and Wes and Delilah debated whether or not they should. Delilah wanted to get moving, but also wanted to enjoy North Platte, and Wes felt the same way, but neither of them could decide.

"Come on you guys," Carmen crooned, adjusting her sunglasses which she wore even though she was indoors. "We can go hiking. Well, maybe not, since you'll be walking a lot as soon as you leave. We can see some of the attractions we skipped yesterday. Check out that old house tour. You know, do tourist stuff."

"I don't know," Delilah said, one of Carmen's hand held mirrors in her palm as she scrubbed dark shadows of mascara from under her eyes.

Carmen didn't seem to have much experience with cross-country hitchhikers, but she decided to give them advice anyway.

"The thing is, with trips like these, you can't be in a hurry," she leaned closer to them over the counter and gestured sharply with rigid hands, "You have to stop and smell the roses. Appreciate America.

That's what cross-country trips are about, not the destination, but the *journey*." She leaned back from the counter to drink her cold pressed juice and stared at Wes and Delilah sternly, in a *come on, do you really think you know better than me* way.

"Well... Wes, what do you think?" Delilah asked.

Carmen turned her full intensity towards Wes. Looking into her sharp, deep eyes, which were gorgeous but also vaguely threatening as she raised her sunglasses, it took a lot of strength to deny her.

"I'm ready to move on," he said.

Delilah sighed. "You know, I guess I agree."

Carmen pouted. "Well, alright then."

Carmen drove them out to the highway and dropped them off with a warm goodbye, their offensive declination of her hospitality already forgotten. They started walking again, and both sighed. The travel was beginning to wear on them. It wasn't that they'd been on the road too long, but they hadn't made as much progress as they were expecting, and they were disturbed by the idea that it could take much longer than they'd hoped to get to Sedona.

It started to drizzle, and then rain, and then pour. The thing about rain is that it's perfectly enjoyable and romantic, but only if there's a dry place and a change of clothes waiting afterwards. Soon they were both soaked through. Delilah tucked the cardboard sign back into her bag. The rain made clothes and hair hang to their skin and dripped from their eyelashes into their eyes, and it ran over their lips and pushed its way into their mouths, and wiping their faces did little, because their hands were just as wet. This was made worse by the knowledge they had no idea when it would end. They hoped the rain would convince someone to take pity on them, but it didn't seem to have any effect. If anything, people were less willing to stop in the rain, and less willing to let wet strangers into their cars. Time began to drag. Eventually Delilah groaned and sat down in wet grass a few feet away from the pavement with a soft squish. Wes joined her.

"I'm already getting sick of this," she moaned.

"Yeah, but you'll get over it and start liking it again. That's how it is with backpacking. You like it, and then you want to go home, and then you're really into it for a while, and then you're starting to hate it but once you get passed that, you feel like you've accomplished something and start having a lot of fun again."

"Seems like it takes a lot of time to get to the fun part," said Delilah.

"Yeah, well there's fun interspersed throughout," Wes said.

It was getting cold, and the rain seemed to be building. They could hear thunder in the distance. Delilah hoped the thunderstorm would pass above them, because it could be sort of fun. She started shivering and tucked her arms closer together.

"Here," said Wes, snuggling close to her and putting an arm around her shoulder, "have some body heat."

"Aww, you're sweet." Delilah wrapped an arm around him and leaned into his side.

It was slightly warmer that way. The thunderstorm did move over them, with cracks of lightning every few minutes, followed by rolls of thunder. Water ran down through their hair and over their faces, down into their clothes and over skin covered in goose bumps. The rain became hard enough that cars couldn't even see them.

"If we can find the nearest town we could at least sit inside a gas station," Delilah said.

"You're right. Let's go."

They got up and started walking again, Wes keeping an arm around Delilah and Delilah keeping so close to him they had to watch their legs so they wouldn't trip over each other. It was miles to the nearest exit. They kept walking. When they reached it, they found a bar and ducked inside, sighing at the warmth as the entered. A sports game was playing on the bar TVs. They sat at the bar wringing rain out of their clothes and drinking water because they couldn't afford anything else, and when one of the sports fans started talking trash about the opposing team, predictably, an opposing team fan started arguing with him. Soon enough the two got into each other's faces, just behind Wes and Delilah.

Wes looked at Delilah and raised his eyebrows, and she rolled her eyes back at him. He pulled her away from the fight, off to a table by the window. Softly but persistently, the rain gathered at the ground in wide puddles that danced with the patter of water, reflecting the neon beer signs as Delilah and Wes watched.

"I do love the rain," Delilah said at the quieter table, tucking her hands near her neck to warm them up.

"Who doesn't?" Wes asked.

"Anyone who can't get out of it."

He decided she was right.

Cheers and boos erupted from the bar as something important happened in a stadium far away. Delilah watched Wes watch the rain, his face glowing in the bar lights. She reached out to his hand that rested on the table, and took it into two of hers, examining it.

"What?" Wes asked.

"I just like hands," she said, turning it over and running a finger over the lines on his palm.

He smiled, face resting in his other hand, watching her hands on his, then flicking his eyes up to watch her downturned face, the way her eyes moved. He reached over to push hair away from her face, over the back of her head.

"What?" Delilah asked.

He shrugged, "I just like hair."

She looked away from his hand, releasing it, into his eyes, and they smiled at each other.

She turned to watch the rain, and then the array of people in the bar, those watching the game and those sitting quietly alone.

"I don't like this place," she said.

"We can leave."

She looked at him and tightened her lips, with an expression saying, *can we though?*

"I mean maybe we could get a ride from someone, drunks are easy to convince," Delilah said.

"That's an awful idea."

"Oh, right, cause of the drunk part, mixed with driving. Damn. I guess we're a little bit stranded."

"There are plenty of twenty-four hour fast food chains. We could hide out in one of those," Wes suggested.

"They'll kick us out if we don't order anything."

"We could hide out in the bathrooms."

Delilah considered that. "Yeah okay. Kari gave me a pack of playing cards. I bet we could make use of those."

"Playing cards in a bathroom, here we come."


They ended up in a handicapped stall of a women's restroom, changing station down and covered with cards.

"Any tens?" Delilah asked.

"Go fish," said Wes.

"How long have we been playing this?"

Wes shrugged. "I don't know, but I'm getting pretty tired."

"Do you think someone is going to clean in here pretty soon?"

Wes nodded towards the toilet, where the water was bright blue with chemicals. "Looks like they already did for the night."

"Oh, of course."

"Want to play something else?" Wes asked.

"Yeah, but I don't know card games," Delilah said.

"We could play war."

"As thrilling and skill-oriented as that game is, I think I'm sick of it."

"Did you play it a lot as a child?" Wes asked.

"Yeah. I always expected it to be fun, and it always disappointed                                                     me."

"Tragic."

"Yeah."

Delilah leaned into the wall, away from the changing station. "Do you think the workers know we're still in here?"

"They've probably forgotten about us."

"I want to go to sleep," Delilah said.

"I don't think we'll get away with that."

Delilah suddenly gasped and straightened up. "Wait, they have a play area here right, with tubes and a ball pit?"

"Delilah, no."

"I bet the workers are all in the back smoking. That's what we did when I worked one of these, and the play thing is only like, ten yards away. We just slip in there, cover ourselves in ball pit balls, and go to sleep."

"Do you really want to sleep in there? We'll probably get horrible diseases," Wes said.

"Nonsense. We'll be fine." She took a deep breath and went to the bathroom door, glancing at the counter. "No one's there. Follow my lead."

She slipped out the door, then gracefully into the play area, and Wes followed. They scooted across the net entrance, up some stairs, down a slide, and into the ball pit which, despite lacking the necessary quantity of balls to completely conceal them, was about two feet deep, which kept them out of sight. They slipped their packs to one side and lay as flat as possible, containing giggles.

"This is insane," Wes said.

"Well, it's working, isn't it?"

"You've got me there."

It wasn't the most comfortable bedding, and the thought of germ laden children chewing on it made Delilah want to gag, but it did keep them dry, and the room was warm, and not *un*comfortable. They did get some sleep, though it was restless and heavily interrupted by long periods of staring up at the net ceiling, wondering how someone could even end up in this position. Overall, the night wasn't too awful.

In the morning they were faced with a new problem.

"Now we have to get out of here," Delilah said, prodding Wes awake.

Wes peered over the edge of the ball pit to the front counter. "Yeah, there are actually people here now. Like, customers."

"You know what, we may just have to swallow our pride and make a dash for it. I mean, worse case scenario is people assume we screwed in the ball pit, if anyone even bothered to look at us. I'm sure we'll be at the highway before anyone tries to do anything about it. And why would they in the first place?" Delilah asked.

"I guess you're right. Let's do this." He stood up and led the way up a tunnel and out another staircase, then out of the glass door and back into the seating area.

Without waiting to see if anyone was looking at them, they slipped outside and headed back towards the road.

"You know, that does make for a fun story. Like, 'this one time I slept in a ball pit.' It sounds cool, right?" Delilah asked.

"It sounds sad."

"Yeah...." She held out a thumb. "Plus, now I want to shower in hand sanitizer."

"I think that would kill you."

"Shut up."

They walked through the fresh, metallic, post-lightening air and began to filter the pit dust out of their lungs. Eyes dimmed and focused downward, lips tightened at the edges, Delilah picked at her nails as she walked and Wes's brow lowered in concern as he noticed.

"I wonder if this is what Lottie pictured. If she thought I'd be traveling with someone else like this, totally broke, doing weird things to stay out of the rain. Or, if she imagined me on a train or plane, someone with money, going on an easy round trip that would only take three days. Maybe she didn't even think of me at all. Maybe she just thought of the first person who would do something for her and scribbled my name on a note to Kari," Delilah said.

"Would you feel differently if you knew?" Wes asked.

"Nah," she said. "But I'd still like to know."

Her voice seemed a bit sad.

Amelia dialed Connor's number and waited for him to pick up. Just as she thought he'd let her go to voicemail she heard the click of the phone being answered.

"... Hello?" His voice was hesitant.

"Hey, Connor... a few things. First, I'm sorry for calling you while high... multiple times... and I'd like to apologize *again* for what happened with the feds."

"Yeah, yeah I've heard this bit before. You didn't mean to throw me under the bus, you didn't do anything against me, really, you just didn't do anything *for* me... I've heard it. I hope you have something else to say, because otherwise this is a waste of our time."

"I do. I do. You know Lottie, the girl who was out here around the time of your arrest? Like, a week before? You kept in contact with her, didn't you?" Amelia asked.

"For a week. I didn't bother trying once I was in prison."

"Hey, don't be ungrateful, I did get you out."

"Dominique got me out, don't lie," Connor scoffed.

"Okay, okay, just-- have you heard *anything* about her? Do you know if she hates me? Did she say anything about me once you left, like if I called her would she be pissed?"

"I don't know. I really don't know, why don't you call her and find out?"

"I just don't want to upset her...." Amelia chewed her nails and stared out the window at the ridges of red in the distance.

There was a long pause on the other end of the phone. Then a click. Amelia swore under her breath.

She kneeled down to stroke the cat that pawed at her pants, and stayed on the floor slowly collecting dust for the next hour, thinking about Lottie, about Connor, Dominique. What was it about her that wouldn't allow her to step in for someone? Why couldn't she just be like them, so caring and poised and... they found joy in things. Not always, but they had moments where their eyes lit up. She could make their eyes light up, but they couldn't do the same for her, and when they really needed it she wasn't there. She hated herself for it.

Finally, someone spotted Delilah and Wes and pulled over to the side of the road. It was a kindly older couple in a dark green, wood-paneled van. The man waved for them to get in, and they did.

"I'm James, and this is Kristi," said James.

"Hey, Delilah and Wes," said Delilah. "We're headed to Sedona."

"That's a lovely area," said Kristi.

"Yeah," agreed Delilah, though she'd never actually been to Arizona or anywhere in the Southwest.

"We'll only be able to take you to Fort Collins," said Kristi.

"Thank you so much," said Delilah, though she was disappointed by how little ground they would cover that day.

"So, what are two kids like you doing on the road?" asked Kristi.

"An old friend of mine died, and we're fulfilling her last request by delivering a box to a family member in Sedona," Delilah said.

"Oh, sweetheart, I'm sorry to hear that. But, my, what an incredible story you'll have," Kristi said.

"We've already had a pretty interesting time." said Wes.

"I'd love to hear more about that," said Kristi. Her voice was a mixture of a Wisconsin and Canadian accent, which made "love" sound like "louve," and "about" sound like "a-boat."

"Well, let's see. We found a dog, and we took it with us to drop off somewhere in the next town, but we stopped at a rest station and it just took off into the woods and we never saw it again," Delilah said.

"My!" said Kristi. "Traveling with a stray dog!"

"And last night we couldn't find a place to sleep, so we just wandered between different bars and fast food places, but ended up in the middle of a bar fight and, well, we got out of there as fast as we could."

"I should hope so! Being in the middle of that sounds scary."

"We got a ride from these two girls whose entire van was filled with succulents."

"How odd, and how intriguing!"

Kristi continued to be enthusiastic while Delilah's voice became increasingly strained as she spoke through drawn lips. James continued to be silent as they drove along the mountainsides, overlooking oblong towns stretched out to fit in deep emerald valleys until they arrived in Fort Collins suburbia, not dissimilar to Kari's white clapboard cul de sac with perfectly manicured lawns and bushes.

"Anywhere you want to be dropped off?" Kristi asked.

Delilah looked out at the dark streets and figured there wasn't anywhere especially ideal, but she looked to Wes.

"By that church, up there, thanks," he said.

"Oh, no problem." It sounded like "oo, noo prooblem," which bothered Delilah, but she tried to ignore it on account of Kristi's kindness.

They got out into the church lawn and watched the van disappear into the night. The church loomed over them in the darkness, an intimidating figure when it wasn't lit.

"Well," said Wes.

"Well," said Delilah.

"This is just as nice a place to spend the night as any," he said.

"I guess so."

They set out sleeping rolls under an outcropping, beneath tall stained glass windows pointing to the heavens. There were some bushes in front of them, which they figured would hide them from the road.

They sat up next to each other and watched the clouds move around the stars.

"What's wrong?" Wes asked.

"Nothing, I'm just tired." Delilah's words fell flat onto the pavement, heavy and limp like wet rags.

Wes scooched in closer to her. He wrapped his arms around her and rested his head on her shoulder. They were silent and unmoving for a while, until Delilah leaned into him and sighed.

"I don't feel okay at all," she said.

"I know."

"Oh, really, what do you know?" She spat the words, and they were sharpened by disdain.

"I know the way people look when they feel like shit."

She closed her eyes and took a deep breath. She moved so her legs were tucked up against the stone wall and her head rested on his lap. He pulled her hair out her face and ran it through his fingers, Delilah relaxing at the soft pull on her scalp, Wes reassured by the warmth of soft curls.

"I sort of wish I was at home," she sighed.

"I know."

"Stop saying that."

"I do though," he said, and she ignored him and continued.

"But, I also really don't want to be home. Ever."

And he felt the same.

"You'll probably feel better sometime," he said, "and then it will seem clearer."

"Sometime I will... sometimes it does... a lot of times it doesn't," she mumbled softly, and he could barely make out her words, "a lot of the times it doesn't seem clear at all, just loud and empty."

Delilah stared at the art on the windows above and said, "I like that their angel windows have curly hair."

Wes looked up.

"But their Jesus is white. And the angels are white too. They always are, and it pisses me off. Also I'm hungry, but I don't feel like eating." She huffed and rolled her eyes.

"Here, have some jerky." Wes dug some out of his pack.

"No, thanks."

"Delilah, you should eat."

"Ugh."

"Please?" Wes asked, holding the jerky towards her.

"Fine...."

"Can I try to cheer you up, or at least distract you?"

"...Fine."

"Alright. My mother was a ballet dancer, so maybe I inherited some of her skill," he stood up and walked a few feet away.

"Oh no."

"Alright...."

"Don't hurt yourself," said Delilah.

"This is called a pirouette," he said, raising one leg up and shakily balancing on one set of toes. That made her smile, though it didn't quite touch her eyes, and shake her head, "Don't even try, I'll dance with you. I know a really basic swing step."

She got up and stood across from him, about a foot apart, taking his hands.

"Here's how it goes... this foot back, then up," she slowly walked him through the movements until they could almost do it, and after a few minutes of giggling and spinning each other Wes sat down and Delilah lay down, her head resting on his lap again.

She fell asleep a few minutes later, but Wes was awake for much longer. He looked down at her and twisted a curl from her hair around his finger. It was so pale it was almost white. Then, after a while, he leaned his head back and fell asleep too.


In the middle of the night, Delilah woke up. She made a short humming sound. She realized she  was still on top of Wes, but didn't move. Did it really matter that her hair was touching his legs? No. Not really, she decided. It wasn't like either of them were turned on by it. She wondered if she should move out of courtesy, just in case Wes wasn't as casual. She decided not to.


Mist hung in the air the next morning, and puddles, softly fashioned by last night's rain, rested in dips of pavement and cobblestone walkways. The church was more visible now, and grey-green walls stretched to barely stand out against the grey-blue sky. The only color in its structure were the stained glass windows, which depicted saints and scenes from scripture. They were surely bright and alive when inside on a sunny Sunday morning, but today their colors were muted and dull, lacking the light source necessary to bring out their artistry.

The city was green and the air was sweet.

They headed off to another day on the road, eating granola bars as they went. That morning they were picked up almost immediately by a younger couple, and dropped off two hours outside the city. From there they had less luck. They did, however, see an interesting dirt path leading off into the mountains. It had a sign reading, "Heritage Farms," with an arrow pointing down the trail.

"Hey, let's check that out," said Delilah.

"I don't know...."

"Come on, are we really in a hurry?" she asked. "Let's just have some fun, explore, tour. Like Carmen said. Don't be a --" Delilah drew a square through the air with her index fingers.

"Don't call me a square."

"I will if you don't come down this trail with me."

"Okay, fine."

They headed off down the trail. It was a nice day, warm but not hot, everything enhanced by last night's weather. Wes pointed to different trees and birds and told Delilah what they were. She listened intently, sometimes pointing to a plant and asking what it was, and he would tell her. Soon, the trail dead ended into a large clearing, three large greenhouses to one side, and little structures dotted here and there on the other, eventually disappearing into the woods. A girl about their age sat, shirtless, on the porch of a small, uneven cottage, smoking a bowl. She was cute, a little bit pudgy, with short black hair and black eyes. Upon seeing them she beamed and called out to them.

"Hey, friends. How'd you find us?" she asked.

"We just followed the trail," Wes said.

"Well... welcome. I'm Tiffany, call me Tiff. You guys look like you could use a... healing environment, no offense. Follow me." She remembered she was shirtless and looked down, "You guys don't mind do you? I mean, I don't wanna upset anyone."

"I don't care," Delilah said.

"It's fine," Wes said.

"Alright, cool. Meadow! There are people here!" She shouted at a cabin a few yards away.

A tall, thin girl with long dark hair and a flower crown came out, dressed in a soft grey dress with nothing under it.

"Oh, hey. Hey, what's up?" she asked.

"We were just exploring," Delilah said.

"We don't normally get visitors. Not many people come out this way. So, what, are you curious about the farm?"

"Yeah. What's up around here?" Wes asked.

"This is all our property. We're, like, what would this be called, a commune? Maybe an intentional community. We've got a population of, I don't know, a hundred maybe. Wait, *Tiff,* is that my weed? What the fuck, stop taking my shit," Meadow said.

"You just said this was a commune!"

"That doesn't mean I can't have my own stuff. Stop doing this! Sorry guys. Want some tea or something? Chris, we have company!" Meadow pushed strings of beads aside from the doorway and led them into a small, a-frame cabin. It had a loft with beds, and the downstairs was living space and a kitchen. The furniture all looked like it had been taken from curbsides, but washed well before being put on display. The floor was covered in light dust, with elaborate but worn rugs over the bare wood, the walls hung with tapestries. There were windows at the front and back of the house, and house plants hugged the sills and were hung from the ceiling in front of them. A man with dark skin, a shaved head, beard, abs, and shorts put a tea kettle on.

"Hey guys," he said, his voice more delicate than his body let on.

"Hey," Delilah said.

The girl named Tiff followed them inside and leaned against a wall, blowing out a cloud of smoke.

"Just dump your packs wherever," Meadow said.

Chris came over with a tea kettle and a stack of cups, and started distributing them.

"A mix of green tea and citrus. I grew everything myself, so you know it's fantastic," he said.

"Thanks," said Wes.

The tea was, as Chris promised, fantastic.

"So, what's your trip been like so far?" Meadow asked.

"Um, it's had its ups and downs. We ran over a dog, on one hand, but on the other I got acrylic nails from a hot college student, so." Delilah cringed at the memory of Ruby and held up her nails.

"Those nails are sick. The dog thing, though, that's fucked up," Tiff said, and, having run out of weed, wiped her bowl off on her shorts and then slipped it into a discreet pocket on the side.

"And now you're here. And you could use a break from the road," Meadow suggested.

Wes laughed, "It's only been, what, four days?"

"Five, if you count today, I think," Delilah said.

"But I bet they were emotionally taxing." Meadow wasn't letting up.

"We really need to cover some ground. I don't know what we'd even do here," Delilah said.

"Meditation. Weed. New age corruption. Chakras. All fun things, that *you two* lucky ducks could be a part of, if you stay a day or two," Meadow said.

"Come on, tourists usually eat this shit up," Chris said.

"We're not tourists," said Wes.

"Then what are you?" Meadow asked.

"My dead ex left me a box, and we're hitchhiking to Sedona to deliver it." She held up the box for Meadow to see.

"That's way cooler than I was expecting. 'Do not open,' what's that about?" Meadow slammed down the rest of her tea and leaned back into the couch, one foot on the armrest and one on the table.

"I don't know," Delilah tucked the box to the side.

"I bet it's drugs. Chris, beer me!" Chris ignored Tiff's request.

"Nah, I bet it's something super personal and you're taking it to their ex-lover, like a box of love letters and dried flowers. I hear some people are into that." Meadow pushed Tiff down as she started towards the kitchen. "Tiff, sober up for a few hours. I mean when was the last time you weren't fucked up?"

"Yesterday. I only do it sometimes. It's just when I do, I go all out, sister."

"You do it too often. And we're not sisters. And put a shirt on!" Meadow took a shawl from the back of the couch and threw it at her.

"You two bicker like a sad, suburban couple who's only staying married because they're imprisoned by society's ways, slowly sinking into a deep hate and resentment of each other that may end in abuse, all of which could be avoided if they would simply get divorced," Chris called.

"Chris is skeptical about the whole 'American Dream' model. We get it, Chris, you're unconventional," Meadow said.

"Damn straight," he said.

"So are we going to get high together or what?" Tiff asked.

"Later Tiff, calm down. I'll give you guys a tour of the grounds. You can meet everyone. If they're not passed out in a river somewhere," Meadow got up.

"If you don't like the way people are, you can leave," Chris said.

"Just saying, some of you guys are a bit too loose for me. Whatever, let's go." She held the door open for Delilah and Wes.

"So!" She clapped her hands together and kept them clasped by her chest, "We are fortunate enough to live in a state where we can legally make a living off weed. I mean, we did it before it was legal, but it's easier now. Over there," she pointed, "are our three greenhouses. Each has a different strain, all very popular. Ours is an honorable heritage. Our predecessors have been working on producing better and better product for decades. Yes, decades. No one lives here more than like, ten years though, the average would be five, mostly twenty and thirty-year-old hippies. People rotate in and out. Alright, let's see some other sites."

They followed Meadow through a small field, towards the assortment of cottages. "These are all hand built from resources found in these woods. No store bought lumber, minimally processed as you can see. No, they're not the nicest and they wouldn't sell, and are certainly not up to code, but they are adorable. Like a house a child builds for a fairy. Ooh, Rowan is here. That means Stella's inside." They approached a cabin with a lean, wolf-like dog lounging on the porch.

"Good girl," Meadow said, patting Rowan as she entered the house.

A tanned, well-built man and a girl with incredible muscles were lounging inside. The house wasn't as cluttered as Meadow's and was better lit, with lots of windows. It was also cleaner, with less dirt on the floor, but still with plenty of hanging tapestries and antlers lining the walls.

"This is Denver. Yes, named after the city. This is Stella. Stella, Denver, this is Delilah and Wes, fulfilling the death wish of Delilah's ex. They're delivering a mysterious package to Sedona."

Stella nodded at them.

"How're the chickens?" Meadow asked her.

"Doing well. Same with the goats and the cow. The fruit trees are coming along nicely," Stella stated.

"Do you mind if I show these guys your farm?"

She shrugged. "I don't care. Go for it."

"Alright." Meadow exited and Delilah and Wes followed.

Meadow showed them past the yoga circle, over a stream, to a small barn and pasture containing Stella's animals. Fruit trees grew along the sides of her grounds, and along the trails that lead to them. It was the kind of place that always had something sweet within reach in the summertime.

"And that's about it. I mean, everyone's individual houses are cool, but I doubt you wanna go to see all of them."

The phone Kari gave them rang, and Delilah twitched in surprise. She pulled it out and put it to her ear.

"Hello?" She froze when she heard the voice on the other end.

"Delilah, where are you?" It was her mother.

"Mom, why are you calling me?"

"You better not be on your way to Arizona." Delilah imagined her mom in her suburban home, now run down and overflowing with useless stuff; antiques that would never appreciate in value, empty cages of long-dead pets, inherited tablecloths and doilies, and a plethora of other junk that had a minute possibility of ever coming in handy.

"I'm in Colorado. I'm hitchhiking to Sedona with a friend."

"Delilah I don't understand you. *That girl* has been out of your life for years and now you're becoming part of a drug circle for her --"

"Mom, it's not about drugs!"

"How do you know?"

"How did you even find me? Why do you suddenly have an interest in me?" Delilah turned to Wes and Meadow and shook her head in anger.

"Kari gave me your number. I'm your mother. Am I supposed to stand by while you throw your life away over your high school mistakes? Give me your location and stay where you are. I'm coming to get you."

"No."

"At least let me come talk to you face to face."

"I have no interest in seeing you, mom."

"I just want to talk."

"Bullshit."

"Delilah...."

Delilah sighed and stayed silent.

"Please," said her mom.

Delilah hadn't seen her mom in a long time. It didn't sound like she had changed, or ever would, but maybe something between them could.

"... Fine. Fine. Meadow, where are we and how can someone find us?"

Meadow gave Delilah directions and Delilah passed them onto her mom.

"I'll be there in two days." Then she hung up, leaving Delilah standing in frustration.

"What was that?" asked Wes.

"My mom wants to talk me out of going to Sedona. I... I don't even know, I haven't seen her since I left home." Delilah ran her hand through her hair.

"Psh. How dare she try to get into your business *now?* Hey, you know what would be fun?" Meadow asked. "Getting your mom high."

Delilah laughed at the thought. "Yeah, she would never smoke pot."

"I'll tell Eugene to make some edibles. He's really good at making stuff that actually tastes okay." Meadow smiled with half of her mouth.

"I'd feel sort of shitty... but it would be pretty hilarious," Delilah said.

"I'm going to tell him to make a batch. Someone will want them regardless."

That afternoon, after guided meditation, Wes and Delilah walked out to a patch of wildflowers together. Delilah sat in front of him, arranging flowers in his hair. She weaved and braided bits of hair around them to keep them in place. She had a few daisies and a pile of small blue flowers, then some dandelions.

"How's it looking?" Wes asked.

"Gorgeous." Delilah sat up on her knees to fasten blue flowers through the sides of his hair.

She looked down at him and stayed there for a moment. Wes reached up and pulled her lips down to his. He kissed her and she kissed back, and it lasted long enough for him run a hand into her hair, and for her to cup her hand under his chin, thumb stroking his jawline.

"That wasn't platonic," he clarified as they broke away.

"I know," she said.

They smiled giddy, preteen smiles and Delilah pushed him back into the flowers and kissed him again, longer this time, and with more intensity. Delilah let him playfully roll so he was on top of her. There, in the middle of a small field of flowers, close enough to the greenhouses to smell weed when a breeze drifted past, they exchanged a real, fire and butterflies kiss. Their lips tasted like the citrus tea they drank in copious amounts after lunch, their breath was just warmer than the air. He brushed his lips against her collarbones just lightly enough for her to feel it and exhaled heavily against her neck and it made her gasp.

And then they laid next to each other, watching the clouds move across the mountains. A few blue flowers had fallen out of the crown when they kissed, and now Wes tucked them back in place.

"Hey Wes," she said, reaching over to draw a thumb over his lips, "I have a question for you."

"You can ask me anything."

"... What's a credit union? I'm part of one and I don't even know what it means because I'm bad at being an adult."

"Delilah...." Wes giggled, "Is that really your question?"

"Yeah."

"That question conflicts with the attitude of this moment," Wes said.

"I'm sorry, do I have to slowly transition into banking to ask these things? I thought we were too close for that. You're already giving me second thoughts about where we stand."

"Yeah, we should probably part ways here."

"If you go home tell the diner where I am, because... I totally forgot to tell them," she said with a laugh of shame.

"You did not!"

She nodded.

"Do you guys wanna get high?" someone called to them.

Delilah looked at Wes and he shrugged. She shook her head. She wasn't in the mood.

"No, thanks," he called back.

"Yeah I totally forgot about that one responsibility," Delilah said.

"Dude. That's bad."

"Yeah, I know."

Wes wrapped his fingers through hers. They watched the clouds for the rest of the day, until Tiff came to find them, just after the sun set and the stars started to come out.

"We're having a campfire. Wanna come?"

"Sure." Delilah stood.

"Help me." Wes held out a hand, and Delilah pulled him up.

"Alright, the fire pit is a bit out of the way. We have to pass through the woods. I'll show you."

Tiff led them out of the clearing and through a short stretch of woods. Another, smaller clearing was filled by a stone fire pit at least four feet in diameter, now with flames rising up three feet above the rim, and a hammock that hung between two ancient looking oaks.

"Everybody, this is Wes and Delilah. Wes and Delilah, that's Damien, Eleanor, Christine, but we call her Tits because there are two Christines. The other one we call Red because she used to be a ginger. Aaron, Ezekiel, and you know Meadow and Chris."

"Hey," Delilah said.

They responded in the same manner.

"We were playing truth or dare," Meadow said. "I hope you don't mind partial nudity."

"I have no problem with that," Delilah said.

Wes shrugged. "Same."

Wes sat on a log and Delilah sat on the ground between his legs, resting her head on his thigh, both unabashed by contact after their kiss. Wes played with her hair and Delilah was calmed by the brush of fingers against her neck and ears. Sometimes she would get lost in the tongues of the fire, the soft movement of cherry glow through the burning logs, and the feeling of Wes in all the places her skin touched his.

"Alright, Delilah, truth or dare?" Damien asked.

She snapped out of a daze. "Dare."

An hour or so went by that way, until the truths and dares began to get boring and conventional.

"Delilah, how come you never pick truth?" Tiff asked.

"Dare is more fun," Delilah said.

"It's easier too," said Chris.

"That's true," Delilah said.

"Do a truth for once," Tiff said. "We're running out of dare ideas anyway."

"Fine. Truth."

"Alright... I can't think of anything...."

"What's your deepest fear?" Red chimed in.

"I'm not answering that," Delilah said.

"That's not how it goes," Red said.

"And now we're really curious," Damien said.

"Fine. I'm afraid of... cockroaches. When I was little I saw a movie where someone ate a cockroach then threw it up and it was still alive. It traumatized me."

"Bullshit," Red said.

Delilah shrugged. "It's the truth."

"Fine, pick someone else."

The truth or dare challenge soon disintegrated into casual chatting. Damien pulled out a pack of cigarettes and started talking.

"So I'm at the doctor's, right? Like, the head doctor. And she asks me all the usual things, you know, am I seeing or hearing things, sad enough that I wish I were dead, angry enough to kill someone, whatever," he paused to light a cigarette, taking a long drag and exhaling forcefully, "and then we started talking about my meds, cause I just got on new anti-psychotics -- which are just mood stabilizers don't worry -- and she asks about paranoia. I have a history of it. I say I'm not paranoid. She keeps asking questions because she doesn't believe me, and I end up saying my friends don't like me anymore. Not you guys, these other jerk-offs who were talking shit about me. She asks what I think the root of my paranoia is. I say I'm not paranoid, I heard them talking shit about me. You want a hit of this?" He held the cigarette out to Red, who took a drag and passed it back. "She's like, 'how many times a week do you experience paranoia?' I'm like, bitch, I'm not fucking paranoid, but of course I don't actually say that. I just said 'no, I actually heard them talking shit about me, I'm not paranoid!' Then she's like 'can you rate your paranoia on a scale of one to ten?' So at this point I'm not going to argue anymore so I'm just like, 'fine, I guess I'm paranoid sometimes, like a six.' She doesn't do anything to my meds. I'm still not paranoid but you bet your ass I don't hang out with Josh and his douche bag friends anymore."

"You used to be friends with *Josh?* Like, the awful Josh, who no one likes?" Red asked.

Damien nodded to Red while people chimed in about their psychiatrists, and Tits called for attention.

"Damien's doctor has nothing on this crazy bitch I saw once. So I go to get a psych eval, right? I go to this lady a friend recommended. She asks me the same questions Damien mentioned, seems legit. Anyway, at the end she says she's diagnosing me with clinical depression, which I figured, so I ask her about prescriptions and therapists and stuff. She says she'd like to try this other thing first, I forgot what it was called. But I ask what it is. She starts talking about how water changes when it's exposed to different emotions. She says 'they did this study where they looked at water that had been exposed to happiness, and it had all these beautiful formations, and then they looked at water that had been exposed to anger and jealousy and other negative things and it was all messed up'-- she didn't say messed up I forgot what she said -- and I'm like... okay? She gives me this tube that you pour water through, and apparently it has all these figure eight tracks inside and it mimics happiness and 'expands the water.' She says it will give me a more positive aura. I'm just like, there's *no way* this person is an actual doctor. So I straight up ask where she got her degree and she says -- no joke -- she was 'enlightened through the power of lucid dreaming'."

"You're lying!" Red said.

"No that's one-hundred percent true, I swear."

"Psh, fine."

"No, really!" Tits insisted.

"Really?"

"Really."

That night Delilah and Wes decided they really needed to take care of their laundry, so they did it together at one in the morning. They stood next to each other outside of Red's house, watching her machines rumble. They stood mostly in silence, but once in awhile Delilah looked over and noticed Wes looking at her, or Wes would look over and noticed Delilah looking at him, and they'd both smile and go back to staring at the washer and dryer. They leaned back on the porch railing, and when their hands brushed against each other they didn't pull away.

They woke the next morning to the two getting ready in the kitchen.

"Sorry, we have to work today," Meadow said. "I'm sure you can find a way to entertain yourselves though, right?"

"Yeah, we'll be fine," Wes responded.

"Okay, I'll see you later then. Go back to sleep."

But it was too light to fall asleep, so Wes and Delilah headed out of the house with Meadow and Chris.

"You could probably go over to Stella's. She'll give you something to do. If you get there soon you might get to help milk the goats," Chris suggested.

Delilah looked to Wes. "Sound good?"

"Yeah, sure."

It was a nice morning, with dew soaking their feet and light mists clinging to their hair. Stella was skimming milk when they got to her house, so they supposed they wouldn't have to learn how to milk goats after all. Wes was relieved.

"Hey. What's up?" she asked as they approached.

"We're here to help with whatever," Delilah said.

"I'm repotting all those succulents." Stella nodded to a porch full of desert plants.

"I can do that," Delilah said.

"There's a stack of larger pots right behind them, along with a mix of soil, sand, and coffee grounds. Don't ruin the plants."

Delilah had an image of Eliza run through her head and flinched internally. She walked over and began teaching Wes how to plant succulents. Delilah always liked the feeling of dirt or sand in her hands, and the soft give as she pressed it into a pot. Wes didn't mind it, but he still tried to preserve his nails, only using the pads of his fingers. Delilah noticed and scoffed at him jokingly. Wes laughed.

It got warm as the day went on, until they were both covered in beads of sweat. Delilah pulled her hair back.

"Oh, you got some dirt on your ear," Wes told her.

Delilah reached a hand, still covered in dirt and smudged it across her ear. "Is it gone?"

"No, let me get it." Wes smeared the dirt farther down her face.

"Oh, now you have some on your nose." Delilah drew a line down his nose and he laughed.

"Stop right there, don't make a mess!" Stella called from the garden.

They smirked and raised their eyebrows in an *ooo, we got in trouble* kind of way, and then wiped the dirt from their faces.

They walked back to Meadow's and found some books. Wes read inside and Delilah walked out to the hammock. She settled in and let out a breath of air in meditation as she stared into the mountains for a moment. She opened the leather-bound book she'd found, which was called "Waiting for the Ballad of Papyrus" and started reading.

Delilah laid on the hammock, book resting softly on her ribs with two towering oaks reducing the soft golden sunlight into individual cascades that fell in small splotches over her skin. Her hair was behaving better than usual and one of her legs hung down, long, soft grass tickling her foot. Wes came out in a light white tee and baggy Hawaiian shorts. Delilah's mouth twitched up with joy, and he returned the expression. He swung into the hammock and wrapped an arm around her, letting her book fall into the grass. She laid a hand on his chest while he hugged her into his side. They laid there until the stars came out, more stars than could ever be seen in a city, or even on the outskirts of a small town in Iowa. They were denser than Delilah had ever seen them. Wes pointed at different stars and named them, and told their stories. Delilah asked if he really knew them or if he was making it all up. He admitted he'd been making it all up, and she laughed into his shirt. They both smelled slightly sweaty but cleaner than usual, and their scent was mixed with that of clean clothes, which neither had been completely accustomed to since their childhood. They fell asleep like that. It got cold during the night, and the dew dampened their clothes and hair, and caused them to cling closer to each other in a search for warmth. They woke with the sunlight at the same time small blue flowers bloomed into it, flowers that were dormant before, but were now scattered all the way into the edges of the trees.

"Hey, is that your mom?" Chris asked back at the house, looking out the window.

Delilah walked over and, sure enough, a thin, pale, hollowed-out shell of a person with dead hair dyed orange was hiking out into the middle of the farm, one hand shielding her eyes from the sun and the other carrying a battered, royal blue suitcase.

"Yeah...." Delilah went and opened the door. "Mom! Over here!"

"What's her name?" Chris asked.

"Mandy."

Meadow brought out a tray of fruity pebble bars and a pot of tea. Tiff came down from the loft to join in the excitement.

"Delilah, this is no place for a girl like you!" Mandy said, after taking one look around.

"How would you know what kind of girl I am?" Delilah leaned against the door frame and waited as her mom staggered towards her.

"Because I raised you, that's how!"

"'Raised.'" Delilah made air quotes as she said the word.

Mandy ignored that and came into the cottage.

"You must be Delilah's mom. So nice to meet you. I'm Meadow, this is Chris. Please, help yourself to some refreshments." Meadow's voice was an octave higher than usual and overly perky, nothing close to its usual drawl.

"I'm Tiff." Tiff was, fortunately, clothed.

"And, mom, this is Wes. I've been traveling with him." Delilah sat down.

"Nice to meet you," Wes said.

Mandy looked in disgust from the informal refreshments to the group's sheer clothing, to Wes, and then to Delilah, who was dressed in her road clothes; a t-shirt and joggers, supportive sandals, and a visible sports bra. Everyone became physically settled, but were emotionally on edge.

"Hi. I'll just have tea, thanks," Mandy said.

"Mom," Delilah said in mock horror, "don't be so rude."

Mandy was visibly upset at the suggestion that she was the rude one in the group, and her throat made a little scoffing sound.

"Mom...."

Mandy sighed and took a fruity pebbles bar. Tiff held back her laughter. Everyone else kept their cool.

"So, mom, you've driven all the way out here to talk to me. What's up?" Delilah cleared a chair for Mandy, and she sat down.

"I was thinking this was a private conversation," Mandy said.

"Does it matter?" Delilah asked.

Mandy sighed, and continued.

"Delilah, I'm worried about you," she said.

"Weird, you don't usually care about me."

"Can everyone just give us a minute? I mean, really." Meadow was the first to stand and Tiff and Chris followed her as she left. Wes took a second longer, looking at Delilah in concern, but when she didn't make eye contact he left with the others. "That's not true, I've always cared about you."

Delilah rolled her eyes.

"Delilah. What's in that box?" Mandy asked.

"I don't know. I'm not supposed to open it."

"You knew Lottie very well. Are you really telling me you have no idea?"

"I have no idea."

Mandy's mouth tightened.

"Fine. Whatever. It doesn't matter. I want you to come back home with me. It's time you got a real job, with a real home and a family. I know I haven't been there for you in a while. But I can't stand by any longer while you let your life slip away. I can help you find a career and find a decent home. But you need to leave everything from this trip here. Delilah, I want to help you... and that starts with telling you that I forgive you."

Delilah reigned in her temper and clenched her jaw to control herself before she spoke. "Alright. I need you to just listen to me for a second. And eat while you're listening. I don't *want* a home in northwest Iowa -- don't interrupt me. Even if you could help, which you can't because you don't even have your own life in order, I don't want it. I am happy with what I have and where I'm going, and I'm going to Sedona. It's not just about Lottie. It's about going on a journey and accomplishing something and if you think you owe me *forgiveness* then you're even more of a deluded waste of skin than I thought. Hey, aren't those bars good?" Delilah asked as her mom took another bite.

"They taste a bit off."

"That's because they come from goat butter. Anyway, how about you just spend the night here, go on your way in the morning, maybe tour Colorado a little bit, and then go back home and focus on fixing *your* life for a change."

"I just don't understand why you're so unwilling to mend bridges back home. You can't hold onto grudges forever. At some point you will have to kiss and make up. You're an adult, for gosh sakes."

"No, I don't have to make up with anyone. I'm working on forgiving them. But that doesn't involve letting them back into my life. Even if they wanted me."

Mandy sighed. "Who else do you have besides your family?"

Delilah shrugged. "Wes. People here, people on the road."

"I mean stable, responsible adults! Not a bunch of potheads! You can't start a family in a trailer park, with someone who doesn't even have a college degree!"

"First, yeah I can and plenty of great people do, but also, these people are stable and responsible. They run a business. Wes is very educated, but we probably won't be starting a family together, not only because we're super casual, but that's not what I aspire too. And to be a pothead you have to smoke multiple times a day, not just on occasion. And everything you just said is insulting to me. There's nothing wrong with my situation. It's better than yours. You know how people said goodbye to me when I left? You know what really stuck with me? The person who told me 'all you queers are going to burn in hell one day.' That's my most vivid memory of home, and if you don't understand why I'm a bit raw about it -- well, it's like I said before. You're delusional. Those things have stuck with me. I'm not going to acquire more hate to carry around, and I really want to be done with anger. Eat the fruity pebbles bar, mom," Delilah said.

"Now listen here--"

"Save it. Don't bring out the mom speech with me. You know you haven't earned that."

Mandy was silent. She knew, on some level, that Delilah was right. Delilah stood up and got a fifth of bourbon.

"Can we just drink and eat together? Maybe not talk about things that will make us hate each other?" Delilah asked.

"We can put this off *for now* but I do intend to finish this conversation."

Delilah held the whiskey out to her mom. Mandy pursed her lips and shook her head, but continued eating the bar, finally finishing it.

"Oh, you realize that bar had pot in it right?" Delilah asked.

Mandy stared at her in shock.

"I thought that was clearly implied. Fruity pebbles bar... at a pot farm... come on, mom."

"You got me high?" Mandy asked in a rage.

"It's your first time so you probably won't be that strongly affected. Wait – that edible was *pretty* potent, so... we'll see."

"That is entirely disrespectful."

Delilah scoffed and teased her, "Oh please, I bet you came here wanting to get high."

"I did not."

"Really?"

"I'm insulted by your insinuation."

"You wanted to get stoned. Figures. It's okay to get high, as long as it's not your daughter, and as long as no one at home finds out."

"I absolutely did not want to experience this."

"Yeah, you did."

"Whatever. I don't feel it anyway."

"Well you're not going to right away, give it forty minutes at least. I'm inviting everyone else back in."

"No, I don't want to be around all of them."

Delilah, though frustrated, honored the request. Mandy pulled out a pack of cigarettes and a lighter.

"I thought you quit smoking," Delilah said.

"I did. Multiple times since you left, in fact." She lit a cigarette and took a drag.

Delilah held out her hand. "Can I have one?"

"I don't want you to start smoking."

"I haven't. I just do it when other people are. I really just like the taste. Though I prefer cigars."

Mandy squinted and didn't move. Delilah stood up and took a cigarette and lighter from her hands.

"You like the taste? So, what, you'd eat tobacco flavored ice cream?" Mandy scoffed.

"Tobacco and menthol, yes, please. I'd wear cigarette smoke as perfume, too, if people knew I wasn't a smoker."

"You just love people thinking you're a degenerate."

"No, I *am* a degenerate, and not because I think it's cool. It comes naturally."

Mandy sat in silence for a long time before responding. "What would it have taken for me to save you from all that?"

Delilah shook her head. "If you'd raised me with more trust in me, with fewer rules and more mutual respect, I think I would have said no to drugs. I still would have said yes to lesbian sex, just not drugs. But I never respected you."

"I know."

More time passed as they waited for the drugs to hit.

"You're surprisingly cool about this," Delilah said.

"Well, I expected no better from you."

Delilah's smile faded. She didn't want Mandy to see the pain her words caused, so she stared up at the ceiling, cigarette butt still held lightly between her fingers. She leaned back towards the coffee table and slowly ground it into an ash tray.

"I'm getting claustrophobic. I'm going for a walk." Delilah headed for the door.

"You can't just leave me like this."

"You'll be fine."

"Delilah... I came here to reconnect with you. I want to hear about the past few years." Mandy's stern demeanor was melting away, and Delilah looked at the face underneath in interest.

She sat down again, facing her mom. "Alright. So... I guess I last saw you the day of graduation."

She told her mom about her fear on the train ride to Michigan. About spending her first nights as an adult in a cheap motel, scared to death about her future. Making friends with the woman who was now her manager, the woman who helped her find a trailer and start a bank account and do her taxes. Delilah talked a bit about Wes, and her other friends, but overall she realized how stagnant her life had been. She arrived at a point of survival, and ground to a halt. She neglected to move up the pyramid away from survival towards something more promising. She filled her mom in on the details of her journey to Arizona, and by then they were definitely both feeling the weed. Not only the lag between mind and body, not only joy's dominance over negativity, not only a comfortingly blank consciousness, but also the body high edibles have a tendency to provide, limbs turned to lead and slow moving relaxation.

"It feels nice, doesn't it?" Delilah asked.

"NO... well, yeah."

"I can't do it too often, 'cause, first, it starts messing up your brain if you do it every day. Also I start feeling bad 'cause I need to think... like, I need my brain to be sharp most of the time. And when I get high every day I'm like, what am I even doing, I'm doing nothing, not even thinking. See, ma, I'm not a total pothead. And it's not as bad as alcohol. In my opinion."

"I don't trust anything that could form habits."

"I'm getting food." Delilah slowly rose up. "Whoa... okay I'm good."

She came back with a plate of vegetables.

"They don't keep any good junk food, only Eugene does that, and he only keeps stuff for edibles," Delilah complained.

"You shouldn't eat junk!" Mandy exclaimed.

"My diet is fine."

"You're really skinny, Delilah."

"I like it that way. I feel pretty."

"Men like a little something to hold on too sweetheart. You're a stick, you need some curves."

"I don't give a fuck what men like, and I don't care about curves. Sure they're hot. Just not my kind of hot. I mean, I like girls with them, but I don't like them on me. I guess I've never had them. But I like this body type. Don't try to control me. You don't have any curves - you wear children's training bras." Delilah giggled for a minute or so.

"I'll have you know I got some very nice, lacy lingerie. For John, in fact."

Delilah stopped giggling. "John?"

"Oh...oh, I didn't think I was going to tell you that. He's not important. Just a guy."

Delilah squinted. "Hold up your hands."

"Why?"

"Because I think you have a fucking wedding ring. Did you get married again?"

"Again? It's only my thir- ah, shit."

Delilah was frozen with shock. "Third? Not second? Third?"

"Delilah...."

"Who was the second? Why is everyone okay with that? Last I heard no one believed in divorce at home."

"People might disapprove... I don't care, *I don't live by their rules.* I was only married to Ralph for a few months. It didn't work out. He was... I don't remember."

"And they say queers are ruining marriage," Delilah said bitterly.

"Excuse me, what's wrong with some change?"

"Marriage is a commitment. You don't marry someone just because you love them. You marry them because you want to spend a life with them. And for the tax breaks. I mean, by all means, get out of a bad marriage, but you have some responsibility for it, like, you know. You have to work a little. Did you just want to have sex with him? Is that's what's going on? Psh, abstinence, ruining the sanctity of marriage."

"I would have thought you'd be all for divorce with your... liberalism... and propaganda..."

"I am! But if you're going to get divorced in a few months don't marry the man!" Delilah grabbed Mandy's cigarettes and lit another one after spending a few moments struggling with the lighter.

"I didn't think we'd get divorced."

"How about a little foresight next time?"

Mandy decided to have another cigarette as well. "We all have our problems. I mean, look at you."

"I assume you're talking about the bisexual thing?"

"What else?"

"Didn't you read the books I gave you?" Delilah asked. "They all talked about historical context and misinterpretations and Hebrew and things?"

"Those books are pure *blasphemy*." Mandy put slurred emphasis on the word.

"Let's stop talking about this, because I can't control my temper when I'm high."

"You didn't mind losing your temper in front of all my friends."

"Your friends were trying to send me to gay camp. That camp closed down, by the way, and apologized for misleading claims. You know mom, for someone who has such a high view of scripture, you're really bad at acting like Christ. I've seen God in a few places, but never in you."

Mandy's jaw dropped. "What are you saying?"

"I'm saying you don't show love. What happened to wearing love over all else? Also you hate poor people. And hookers. Or anyone who's not like you. And you have a dictational view of the Bible, which... I just generally dislike about you."

"I don't hate poor people."

"So you do hate hookers? Jesus had deep conversations with prostitutes, you know. He recognized their potential and sent them away to spread his message. He didn't scoff in horror."

"You're so high and mighty about religion. You're a hypocrite. You don't tithe, you don't feed the poor, you don't do anything."

"I let homeless people sleep in my trailer all the time. *ALL* the time, mom. I know it's not safe. I haven't had any problems though, I mean I've been robbed but I don't keep anything of value. I haven't been attacked, but if I were, I keep pepper spray under my pillow. I try to be nice, and I try to keep people from feeling bad about themselves. I talk about my religion. I still suck at it half the time. I'm not saying I'm the model Christian or anything. I'm just saying people like you are the reason my generation is so cynical about it."

"You're arrogant. You say you aren't but you are," stated Mandy.

"Whatever. I can't think clearly enough to fight with you right now."

Mandy stood, swayed for a few seconds, then headed for the door.

"Be careful on the steps," Delilah called after her.

The others must have been waiting outside, because as soon as she left they came in. Wes looked at Delilah's expression with concern.

"You okay?" he asked.

"I'm just *fine,* darling," she said.

"You shouldn't have drank with that pot. Those edibles were pretty potent," Meadow said, seeing the bourbon on the end table.

"I'm fine," Delilah said again. "I'm not even that high."

"So, is your mom going to stay the night, or was this just a day trip?" Chris asked.

"It'd be insane to drive all the way out here just for that... though I suppose she now remembers why she hasn't visited me all these years. She'll probably head to a hotel for the night, visit something historical, make a trip out of it and forget we ever talked."

"Why'd she even come out then?" Meadow asked.

"Because she wanted to reconnect, 'cause she felt guilty and didn't want me to get tied up in some sort of drug ring. I don't know. She wanted to feel like a mom again. Get me that bourbon."

"Delilah, I think you're good where you are," Chris said.

"I haven't drank in a long time. I just want to get wasted for once." She looked at them pleadingly.

"Whatever. But Wes is your babysitter for the day, not us." Chris picked up the bottle of whiskey.

"Delilah, you shouldn't drink right now," Wes said.

"You can't stop me," Delilah snapped.

"I'm not going to physically take the bottle away, but I really don't think you should," Wes said.

Delilah held her hand out to Chris for the bottle, and he gave it to her. Wes looked disapproving but didn't stop her. Meadow and Chris went out together to do something that didn't involve a sad, cross-fading hitchhiker, and Wes settled down across from her.

"Are you sure you want to drink that?" he asked.

"I am so sure," she said briskly.

She couldn't process what she was feeling in this state, she just knew she didn't like it, and it reminded her of other feelings from over a year ago. She took a sip of bourbon, and when it did nothing to ease the turmoil her mother had stirred inside her, she took another.


Later, Wes tried to take the bottle away from her, and she snapped at him and held it closer.

"Don't try to control me," she said.

"I'm not trying to control you. I just want to make sure you're taking care of yourself," he said.

"Well, stop."

"Delilah, please. You need to sober up."

"You don't even know me."

He became silent. He watched her rustle around on the couch, hands pawing at her hair, trying to organize it, eyes drooping and lip lips parted slightly.

"You don't."

He didn't respond.

"I MEAN IT."

"Yeah, I know. I heard you... Delilah, come on. You're not okay, you need to stop."

"Fuck off."

"*Delilah,* come on," his voice built, but he cut himself off and sighed, resting his head in his hands while Delilah took another sip of whiskey.

Delilah looked over at him and narrowed her eyes. He shook his head at her again.

"Well, Wes, tell me all about it. Tell me all about the fucked up person you're projecting onto me," she said, her intuition showing itself despite the influence of narcotics.

"What?"

"Who couldn't you save? Whose face hovers behind my eyes when you see me in pain, because no, you don't want to save me, no one really wants to save me, Wes... someone is in your mind. Someone you're really trying to help but it's too late now, too late to save them, you're stuck with me, my disfunction now and it's all going to end the same way. Who couldn't you save?" She shook her head at him, then turned away to stare at the couch cushions. And she was right. Wes saw someone else in her.

Wes had a brother whose hair was like the ocean in the unruly patterns of its waves, and his eyes were like the sky. Four years younger than Wes, he wasn't around to see his parents thrive, only to watch them disintegrate the way kindling does in a fire, and it must have done something to him because he turned out the same way. The alcohol, and that anger that sits right on top of someone's heart and just below their skin. Wes watched him turn from a little boy to a man who was no more mature, just stronger, just more powerful in terms of self-destruction. This was the brother he had found the December after his mother's death, wrists slit on the bathroom floor with blood running between tiles, black in the dark, crimson when Wes turned the light on.

Later that afternoon Mandy dropped by with her suitcase in hand.

"Wes," she said, "could you please give us a moment?"

Wes looked at Mandy and pursed his lips. "Yeah, sure."

She shook her head at the sight of her daughter sprawled out on the couch, so far gone, so far from her usual sharpness.

"You know, when I came I was hoping you had changed. I thought maybe this trip would be your way to let go of the past before you actually made something of yourself. But, you're just as stubborn and resentful as you've always been, and it's keeping you from growing up. I'm leaving now, Delilah. If you want to make anything of yourself, you need to give all this up. All the narcotics. And all your old feelings for Lottie. You'll turn around and go home, if you know what's good for you."

"Yeah, mom. Okay. You know... I know I haven't been good enough for you. I know I haven't done enough or become anything and I'm sorry. I'm so sorry. I'm embarrassed and I'm sorry, and I'm a failure, I know." She paused to cover her mouth as it quivered, and stared at the beams above her before continuing, "But this is something I NEED to do, for her and for myself, and for Wes because I want to do this with him. I like him, mom. And we're going to Sedona, and I'm not asking for your help. I'm just asking you to tell me you're okay with it, or with *me,* because as fucked up as you are, you're still my mom and I still have an illogical desire to make you proud somehow, and now that's impossible for me... but just don't be ashamed of me anymore. I'm smart. I'm pretty. I have a boyfriend, sort of, and I'm doing a hipstery adventurous thing. Please when you go home, don't talk shit about me. Don't frown at your new husband as you tell him how much of a wreck I still am, because I can't handle it. I can't handle having that image in my head. I can't take it anymore. I can't think about it anymore. Please mum." Delilah's eyes, watery throughout her speech, spilled over and she clumsily wiped away a tear.

"Delilah. You're not sober."

"That means I'm telling the truth for once. Because my whole life I've been dead honest with everyone except for you. Why? I guess I didn't want to get into any more trouble. But also because I care about you too much to tell you the truth. Because it would break your heart. Because you don't know the half of it. If you knew everything I did it'd tear you to shreds, either from love or shame. And I'm selfish, and I didn't want to feel guilty for that."

"Delilah...."

Delilah held her hands to her head to hide her tears.

"I'm heading home. Do what you want." And Mandy was gone with her royal blue luggage.

At that, Delilah broke down and fell into the couch face down, sobbing brokenheartedly. Despite every logical argument she set up for herself, something in the voice of her mother cut through it, straight to her center. It cut into her and told her to look at her soul and see its worthlessness. Look into those metallic blue eyes and see gun barrels, see nothing but the dark edge. Look at her scars, and see they're too shallow to release the fog that stalks through her veins. She was drunk, and still a little high, eyes bloodshot and puffy.

Wes saw her. He almost turned around and walked out, but didn't. He almost said how right he was, but he stopped himself. He walked in and sat down on the couch next to her, resting a hand on her shoulder, giving it a little squeeze. Delilah kept on crying.

She came down late that afternoon and slept it off while Wes repacked and replenished their stores of food for the road. The next morning they were ready to head out again, Delilah fortunate enough to have avoided a hangover, other than a mild stomach ache.

"Since you guys are heading to Arizona anyway, could you make a little delivery for me? It's in Prescott, it's not far from Sedona. There are some friends of mine out there. They've already paid. I told them I'd send someone out there when I got the chance." Meadow reached into the cabinet and pulled out a gallon bag half full of weed.

"That's a lot of pot," Delilah said.

"Indeed. And if you smoke it I'll know, and I won't be happy, got it? Good. I'll stuff it in a tampon box, just in case you get stopped by someone. I really doubt you'll have trouble, and no one's going to look at you too closely. You should be fine."

"Are you okay with that, Wes?" Delilah asked.

"I don't have a problem with it," he responded.

"Alright then. Put it somewhere in my pack, Meadow."

"Okay, and I put a piece of paper in there with the address, too."

"Bye, you guys," Wes said as Meadow and Chris saw them out.

"Yeah, thanks for everything," Delilah said.

"Bye. It's been nice having you," said Chris.

"Absolutely." Meadow said, then addressed Delilah. "Hey, also; you're a badass. Don't let anyone fuck with you, alright? Even if they're family."

"I won't. Thanks again, Meadow."

They headed out, laden with their packs, and began walking down the mountain road, thumbs up. The mountains were green, and the air was bright and crisp.

"There aren't as many people on this highway. I'm not even sure exactly where we are," Wes said.

"Yeah, me neither. But we're heading southwest, sort of, so I think we're good."

"Get the map out."

Delilah pulled it out and examined it. "Okay, let's find someone and ask for directions to Aspen, and we'll go from there."


Before they saw another vehicle they came across an impressive mansion, artfully constructed with smooth, pale wood and large panels of glass and charcoal colored stones. It sat at the top of a gradual slope, the lawn left wild and bordered by pines.

"That looks expensive," Delilah said. "Do you think they'd give us money?"

Wes laughed. "We might as well check it out."

They started up the driveway until they saw an old man sitting on a log bench outside the house, who appeared to be asleep. The two stopped a few yards short of him.

"Should we wake him up?" Delilah asked.

Wes considered it for a moment. "Yeah."

"Excuse me?" Delilah said loudly.

"Sir?" said Wes.

"*Sir?*"

Wes walked forwards but stopped as soon as a breeze wafted the man's scent his way. He covered his mouth and gagged.

"Um," Wes choked out.

"Holy shit." Delilah ran up and poked the man's shoulder.

He fell from a seated position down onto the bench.

"He's dead." Wes said.

"Yikes."

"Yeah."

"Well...." Delilah paused.

"Should we call someone?"

"Who?"

"9-1-1?"

"Maybe...." Delilah walked forward and began rummaging through the man's pockets.

"Delilah, what are you doing?"

"He's dead and rich, he can spare --" She found his wallet and counted the cash inside. "Eighty dollars."

"You're robbing a dead man."

"I would argue that it's more moral than robbing a living one."

"It's wrong."

Delilah looked at the money in her hand. "This could get us a bus to Arizona. Or a cheap hotel. Or a really nice meal. It's a good idea to keep some cash on hand."

"This is making me really uncomfortable."

"More uncomfortable than sleeping in the rain in the middle of the mountains and ending up mauled by a bear in a ditch somewhere, only to be discovered by a group of boy scouts – sorry, star scouts -- three months later?"

"You're upset, and it's making you reckless," Wes stated.

"Oh, really? You know that, do you? Wes, I get why you'd feel weird about this. I do. But honestly, who's it going to hurt? His family, or whoever he's leaving his stuff too, is getting all this, what's eighty dollars going to do for them?" Delilah asked.

"It's fundamentally wrong."

"Well, do you want to take it or not?"

Wes ran his hand through his hair. "No... but we do need it... I guess. I guess we can take it."

Delilah slipped it into her bra, and looked back at the house. She trotted up the steps to the door and tested to see if it was open. It was.

"What are you doing now?" Wes asked, exasperated.

Delilah looked over her shoulder at him. "I just wanna see what it's like on the inside."

He shook his head, but followed her. The home had no interior walls, and was almost all natural light and pale furnishings, with oak floors and rustic decorations. Delilah headed towards the stainless steel kitchen and opened the fridge.

"Are you kidding? Delilah, you need to calm down, and we need to hit the road," Wes said.

She pulled out a baggie with three marinating steaks.

"It'd be a shame to let these go bad," she said.

Wes was silent.

"I mean, they're probably really expensive, and they've been marinating for who knows how long, and I am quite competent with a grill," Delilah said. "But, if it makes you uncomfortable, I'll put them back."

"Delilah, what the *fuck* is going through your head right now?" Wes sounded legitimately angry and Delilah was taken aback.

"I'm not sure," she said. "I'm really not. But, Wes. Just think. There's no reason not to."

"Yes, there is," his voice grew heavier and sharper with each response, and his brow furrowed further.

"The dead man is dead. What, are we disrespecting him? Do you think he'd be upset, because I doubt it. We're in the mountains, no one's going to catch us. What's going through my head, I don't know entirely. I don't think about things as they're seen anymore. I think about them from my point of view... am I making sense?"

"Don't grill the steaks," Wes said.

Delilah frowned. "Fine. I want to see the rest of the house though."

"Fine." The word fell hard and broke as it landed, like glassware.

The upstairs was similarly styled, but not as open, with two bedrooms, a large bathroom, and a whole apartment complete with a bed, bath, and kitchenette. There was a long room with one wall made completely of glass, emerald tinted sunlight streaming through it, and every other wall was covered in book shelves. Delilah threw her pack on the ground and Wes followed suit.

"This is too amazing. I want to live here," Delilah said.

"Too bad the owner is laying dead out on the front bench."

Delilah laughed at how ridiculous that was, then felt guilty, then ignored it. "Yeah, guess I can't buy it from him."

Delilah began checking out the books, occasionally taking one off the shelf and flipping through it.

"I haven't read in a long time. I used to read all kinds of books. I loved *The Great Gatsby*. And *The Bell Jar*. I was such a high school girl."

"Those are very good books," Wes said, "Now I think we should go."

Delilah turned and watched the wind move the branches of the pine trees. Delilah jolted as she heard a scream.

"Shit," she said, and ran to look out a window on the other side of the house.

A couple had driven up and found the dead man, the man sobbing hysterically while the woman held his shoulders and covered her mouth. Another car was pulling up, and another couple ran out, the husband hanging back to tell two young girls to wait in the car.

"Shiiiiiiiiiit!" Wes said.

"Let's sneak out the back and run through the woods, and then back to the road," Delilah said, trying to maintain control over herself.

"They'll see us! There's nowhere to hide the entire house is glass!"

"Well – okay... come on!" Delilah grabbed his hand and ran away from the window.

"Where are we going?"

"I don't know, someplace that isn't half windows." The pitch of her voice rose as she ran to the library where they left their packs, shoved one to Wes, and pulled him into the bathroom, carefully shutting the door behind them.

"We can't just stay here," Wes said.

"Do you really think they're going to be checking out the whole house? They might not even come in. Here, if I look from this angle I can sort of see them. They're just standing around calling someone. They can't see us." She took deep breaths as she reassured herself.

"They'll be here for hours probably. They have to call the coroner, and I don't know what else they'll need to do but they aren't just going to leave his dead body lying there," Wes said.

"Okay, but once the body is picked up they aren't going to linger, they'll go back to someone's house and have a family gathering or something," Delilah said, peering out the window again.

"Unless they have it here."

"Where they found the body? That sounds painful for those mourning."

"Well, I guess we'll find out." Wes sat down on the tile floor while Delilah continued to watch the gathering outside. He watched her, her rapid, shuddering movements and the way fear slipped past her defense every once in awhile.

"Oh, shit," she said after a few minutes. "Shit, shit, shit."

"What?"

"The first woman who showed up just sent everyone inside, probably to wait for whoever they called to arrive," Delilah said.

"Well, I doubt they'll come upstairs," Wes said.

"Unless someone has to use the bathroom."

"Is there a bathroom downstairs?" Wes asked.

"There's a bathroom downstairs, isn't there? I mean this is probably a million dollar property. There's gotta be a bathroom downstairs," Delilah said.

"I don't know, I don't remember."

They heard footsteps ascending the stairs.

Delilah lowered her voice to a whisper and stretched her eyes wide while her eyebrows scrunched. "Oh, fuck! Wes, what do we do?"

Wes grabbed her arm and led her into the bathtub, then pulled the curtain shut around it and sat down across from her. They heard footsteps moving down the hall, and muffled voices speaking softly, accompanied by gentle crying. They couldn't quite make out what people were talking about.

The bathroom door opened. Delilah and Wes both covered their mouths. The door shut, and the toilet lid clanked open. Delilah and Wes raised their eyebrows at each other.

"As if this day wasn't bad enough." A voice that sounded like it had just been crying called to someone outside, "Marie, do you have a tampon?"

Someone called through the door. "I have a pad."

"Can I have it?"

"Sure, I'll slide it under the door."

Delilah just shook her head at Wes, horrified. Wes closed his eyes and returned the gesture. She crossed her arms over her chest and mouthed *this is so fucked up.* Wes nodded. They heard the crinkling of paper, and a bit later the toilet flushing and the sink turning on. A zipper opened, and some cosmetics knocked against each other until the lid of a lipstick popped off, and then on, and a zipper closed. The door opened and closed again.

"I can't believe this...." The voice outside receded down the hall.

Delilah softly let out a breath of relief. The door opened again and she rolled her eyes in frustration.

"Where did you say it was?" It was a man's voice now.

"Under the sink," a woman's voice called.

"I'm not seeing it."

"Then check the drawers."

"Still nothing," he said.

"Well, they have to be *somewhere,*" she called.

"Christine, why do you care so much about his essential oils?"

"They're from France, and very expensive."

"Damn it Christine, could you let the body cool before you start raiding his house?" Footsteps stomped out of the room and the couple started fighting as they walked back downstairs.

"We've gotta get out of here," Wes whispered.

Delilah nodded, but whispered back, "How?"

Wes opened the curtains a bit and peered out. "Follow me."

"*Wes,* they'll catch us."

"No, they won't, it'll be fine. And if they do we'll just sprint for the woods."

"I don't think this is going to be fine."

"Don't panic, Delilah, I've got this."

"I'm going to have a panic attack." Delilah's voice grew shrill.

"Here, stay calm. Just breathe for a second."

Delilah closed her eyes and breathed slowly. She held her hands to her collarbones and opened her eyes again, though still panicked.

"Let's go," she said.

Wes creeped out of the bathtub and checked both ways before slipping out the door. He waved for her to follow him. They tiptoed down the first three stairs, before the stairwell opened into the ground floor. Wes peeked around the wall and saw the family standing in the living room.

"Is that Mini's car?" a woman asked angrily.

"Dammit, why would you call those two?"

"His grandpa just died!"

"So, he brought his fiance. Is he insane?"

"Well, she certainly is," a teenage girl with pink hair and a band tank mumbled.

"Leave her alone for once, Tina." A man in a dark grey suit with silver hair who looked like he might be Tina's father scolded.

The front door opened.

"Hey, Jeff," the woman who had originally noticed Mini's car said sadly.

The conversation quieted down to civil mourning, until the woman wearing a body con dress and platforms who had walked in with Jeff, presumably Mini, jumped in.

"Oh, and the wedding. How terrible! It's going to ruined!" she said.

"Can you forget the wedding for five seconds? Jeff's grandfather was just found dead!" It sounded like Christine.

"I'm just thinking it's a shame he won't be there!" said Mini.

"You're thinking it's a shame you can't use his property for the reception anymore!"

Delilah looked at Wes, mouth agape.

"How dare you --"

"No, I'm done with you, you bitch. Jeff I'm disappointed in you --"

"We're in love!" Jeff shouted.

*"She only loves you for your money. Are you blind?* ARE YOU REALLY THAT STUPID?"

"I'M NOT A GOLD DIGGER!"

"You're so goddamn fake!"

"What's that supposed to mean?" Mini asked.

"Your hair is all extensions because you killed the real stuff with bleach, you talk an octave higher than your natural voice, your name isn't even Mini, it's Wilhelmina!"

"I'm sorry for having a nickname!"

Delilah looked back at Wes and shook her head, mouthing, *this is gold.*

Wes just nodded. There was more shouting until finally they heard the sound of something large and made of glass shattering against a wall. Silence fell.

"You motherfucker," someone said softly.

The room erupted in shouts again.

*Let's just run for it,* Wes mouthed.

Delilah hesitated, then nodded. She held up one finger, then raised a second, then a third, then sprinted down the stairs with Wes close behind. Without looking back they charged for the patio door, running straight into a quieter sector of the family who blocked their way.

"And who are you?" some teen in a muscle tank and cargo shorts asked, looking like a white-trash college DJ due to his long greasy hair and name-brand sandals worn over socks.

"Oh... well..." Wes began.

"Well, sir," said Delilah, "you would not believe the day we've had."

The rest of the family now noticed them and the focus of their shouting and threats switched from each other to Delilah and Wes.

"Stay where you are. I'm calling the police!" said Christine, who was too thin for her height and overly made up, like a toy giraffe a young girl practices her cosmetic skills on.

Tina's father was already on the phone with the cops.

"Now, look, we have a legitimate reason for being here," Delilah said. "And I am about to explain what that is... would you like to start, pal?"

Wes looked back at her desperate glance and opened his mouth for a few seconds before speaking. "Well...."

"Okay, fine, we're on a road trip and we just wanted to check the house out, okay? Nothing sketchy. We aren't robbing it we were just curious, I swear, we're very sorry," Delilah said.

"So sorry."

"Also, our condolences. Very sorry for your loss."

"I'm sure he was a great man," Wes said.

There was a long period of silence.

"The police are on their way," Christine said.

"Hey. Let's not get anyone who doesn't need to be involved involved in this. This is between us, and your family. The government doesn't really have a place here," Delilah said.

"I don't think we're getting anywhere," Wes mumbled.

"You two --" The speaker didn't get to finish because Wes burst into action.

He leapt through the quiet sector of the family, pushing them aside and flinging the patio door open as Delilah sprinted through, then passed her as she threw the picnic table on its side and flung the chairs in the route of their pursuers before taking off towards thicker brush.

Wes and Delilah kept sprinting until they put the lawn far behind them, moving unusually fast considering the weight of their packs, and pushed on until they were a safe distance into the woods. Delilah shoved her pack to the ground and leaned against a tree, panting for breath. Wes did the same.

"My lungs... they burn," Delilah gasped

"My legs... are about to collapse..." Wes responded.

Delilah sunk to the ground and rested her head between her knees.

"You okay?" Wes asked.

"Just give me a few minutes to get over this."

She sat and breathed deeply, focusing on each inhale and exhale, listening to her heartbeat repeat itself over and over. After a minute or two Delilah giggled, and Wes giggled, and then they both started laughing so hard they couldn't catch their breath. It started as loud guffaws, then grew completely silent while tears streamed down their faces. Delilah rolled onto the ground and clutched her stomach. Wes fell next to her. They both started to gather themselves.

"Heh, ahh..." Wes fell silent, but then giggled again and it started all over.

Finally they laid side by side, sighing.

"I can't decide which was worse; Ruby, or that whole mess," Delilah said.

"I don't know, it's pretty close. I'd go with Ruby, probably."

"Oh... now I'm sad, poor Ruby."

"Gosh, what time is it?" Wes asked.

"Time to get a watch," Delilah said sarcastically.

"Shut up. Really."

"I don't know," she said.

"Wow, I'm getting eaten alive by mosquitos."

"We should find the road again." Delilah stood up and swung her pack onto her back.

"Yeah, I guess."

They walked in a line they figured was parallel to the road until they thought they were a safe distance from the house, then walked back towards the pavement.

"That family, though," Wes said.

"Oh my gosh, how are they not on TV?" Delilah laughed.

"I guess everyone's family is some degree of messed up."

"True."

The road bent downwards until they were walking beside a river. There was standing water where the earth dipped.

"I bet this river flooded earlier," Wes said.

"Probably," Delilah said.

She swatted away a group of flying bugs larger than gnats, but they gathered around her again.

"Oh, no. Black flies," Wes said.

"I don't think I've had a problem with black flies before," Delilah said.

"Lucky us. We're about to experience it."

Mosquitoes also started to land on them. Delilah blew a fly away from her mouth. Her hair blew in front of her face and she saw bugs were getting caught in it.

"Ew..." she said.

"Damn it." Wes waved his arms around his head, but the flies didn't seem to mind.

They kept walking, swatting as they went. Delilah scratched her ear and dried blood chipped off.

"Ew, what even..." she groaned.

"Yeah, they bite you and sometimes just die on you. I don't know if it's guts or blood or what, but it gets crusted behind your ears if the flies are really thick."

"I hate this." Delilah scraped blood from behind and inside her ears, then under her bra straps. She brushed swatted fly carcasses off her neck, and picked them out of her hair, but they were soon replaced by more carcasses.

Wes started running and Delilah joined him, but the flies, though inconvenienced, kept up.

"I'm diving in the river!" Delilah yelled.

"No, they'll swarm you more if you're wet!"

"I'll swim underwater!"

"What about our stuff?"

"We'll keep it above the surface, and the packs are water resistant anyway. It'll be fine!" Delilah said.

"That's going to be difficult."

"I can do it."

"Okay, go for it."

They ran for the river and jogged in, laying flat on their stomachs so their packs only got wet along the edges. They let their bodies, carefully kept underwater, float along with the current, only their heads and packs peeking out.

"Yes! They're leaving us alone!" Delilah shouted.

The flies began to reform around them. They dipped their heads under for a bit and then came back up. They continued on that way until rapids appeared up ahead.

"Think we should try to make it through those, or just get out?" Delilah asked.

"Definitely get out." Wes swam towards shore and, once there, pulled Delilah out after him.

Delilah spat some river water out of her mouth.

"I think my stuff is fine," Delilah said as she caught her breath and checked her pack.

"Yeah, mine, too."

At that moment, thunder cracked overhead.

"Oh, are you kidding me?!" Delilah shouted as a downpour began.

"Hey, at least the flies will leave us alone," Wes said.

"Ugh, I'm itchy, I still have flies in my hair, I'm wet and my stomach hurts and now mud is sticking to me. I feel so gross right now."

"Just think of the rain as a sort of shower."

Delilah groaned.

As they walked it started to get dark. They kept walking.

"What are we going to do for the night? There's nowhere to sleep, and I don't want to sleep like this anyway," Delilah said irritably.

"We'll just keep walking." Wes's voice was impatient.

Delilah groaned and scratched at a mosquito bite.

"Don't scratch them," Wes said.

"Shut up."

"Delilah."

"I'm not in the mood for this right now!" Delilah snapped.

"For what?"

"I don't know, for you."

"I'm sorry, what did you expect this trip to be like?" Wes asked.

"Just...."

"I don't know why I even let you drag me into this," Wes snapped, and stopped walking, turning towards Delilah.

"Yeah? Drag you from what, what would you rather be doing right now?"

"I'd rather not be in the middle of nowhere soaking wet and hungry and exhausted – and dirty -- in the middle of the night, covered in bug bites and scratches and interacting with one human being."

"Wes." Delilah sounded frustrated, but was hurt.

"I don't even know why we're doing this. You haven't even seen Lottie in years and she left you that package with no explanation. She's your high school girlfriend, and no one approved of you. Of course you remember her as the love of your life, but do you even remember why you were together? Or were you just the only two openly queer girls in northwest Iowa?" His voice grew louder and faster.

"Oh," Delilah breathed.

She paused and turned out to look at the road, then up into the rain to see the clouds. She snapped back towards Wes, and regained the strength in her voice as she responded.

"Why do you think this isn't worth anything? Do you really think I'm only doing this because I loved her? Are you stupid? I have been *miserable* and stuck in one place or another my entire life, and I've barely seen anything or done *anything* unique or exciting. Going back home just made me angry at the world all over again, and Lottie losing to herself made me angry. I just wanted to get away from myself, and my life. I'm running away, Wes, not just fulfilling a last request. And I brought you because you were there, and I didn't want to be alone."

Wes was quiet. Delilah locked eyes with him, straight faced and unflinching.

"So you just brought me because I was available?" he asked.

"What, you think you were somehow special, or I *chose* you for something? No, I'm not special enough to gift you with my presence. *This,*" she gestured at the two of them, "is just how it happened. And don't try to tell me you really saw something in me. What could I give you other than a distraction? I mean really, why else would you do this with me?"

"Delilah, what are you saying? Why don't you think you're worth anything? I go to that shitty diner for a reason, and it's not for the free cardboard crackers or shit coffee. I ask you about your schedule and find a way to get there when you work because I like seeing you, and talking to you-- no, forget about me. Delilah, you're worth so much, and the way you've been acting in just the past day is really making me worry about you."

Delilah cupped her face in her hands and looked down at the ground through her fingers. The grass was giving way to mud, and the earth sank beneath her, lowering her by at least an inch. Her shoes had become soaked through, but she was starting to ignore the water.

She looked up at Wes again, into his eyes. "That's stupid. That's so fucking stupid."

Wes reached a hand up to run it through his hair, and Delilah, seeing his hand rising, flinched instinctively. Wes saw it and froze.

"Delilah..." he said, "Delilah, oh my God."

"What? It's nothing, really."

"Delilah."

Delilah covered her mouth as she started to cry, "No, it's nothing, don't worry about it."

"What happened?" Wes asked, gently placing a hand on her waist and the other under her chin.

She pulled away and he stepped back. She wrapped her arms around herself.

"Just... ugh I just hate it, Wes. It was, you know... high school. Just leave it."

"Delilah..."

"No, I don't want this. I don't want everything between us to be you babysitting me after you find out yet *another* reason I'm... the way I am. I'm tired of every relationship I have ending with someone taking care of me or fucking me over. I don't want you to know about everything. Just drop it. I mean, there's no way you *want* to hang out with someone having a breakdown."

"Delilah, I haven't been babysitting. You've given me so much, and you're a bit unstable sometimes. My life is a bit too monotone sometimes, and we compliment each other. You can tell me anything you want to. I might not understand everything, but I'll accept it and won't patronize you for it. I swear."

Delilah shook her head and rolled her lips against each other

"My dad..." she looked down, then back up, "he was never that stable and then all this shit happened... Lottie and me." She looked down and shook her head. "Okay. Okay. Wes, I come from a long line of mental illness and alcoholism and my family got really ugly sometimes. Okay? But the thing that really pissed the family off wasn't the man who beat his wife and daughter, and it wasn't the girl who went to prison for fraud, it was that one cousin who 'decided to become gay'. I'm so serious right now, I'm the family exile, not him. Well. I guess I didn't stick around to give them a chance to change their mind about me. Still, I doubt it would have done any good. And everyone who's heard about that gets that look on their face, like *oh, sweetheart, so precious, I must save you you poor little victim* and I hate it. Or-- *or* they don't do that. They go *how could you leave your family you little heathen* and I'm not sure which is worse. Or they act like they don't care, but then later they throw it all in my face, or they act accepting and then later they ask how I'm not over it by now, or why can't I learn to control my depression or my panic because they think I can somehow control a physical illness just because it's in my brain. Just... my dad... it wasn't a fun household."

She moved closer to him again.

"Delilah, you know I'd never..." he trailed off.

"Beat the shit out of me? Yeah, Wes, I know. Instinct, or muscle memory, it just kicked in for a second. And my dad's long gone, he drank himself to death after he left my mom... I don't need to worry about it anymore. Come here." She held her arms out for a hug, and Wes accepted.

"I'm sorry, Delilah," he said.

"Hey. You didn't do anything."

"I'm sorry it happened to you."

"Yeah, you should have seen some of my friend's families," she said bitterly.

"I'm still sorry it happened to you."

"This day has really been something," Delilah sighed.

"Delilah, I know you don't want to hear it but I was serious when I said I'm worried about you."

"No, don't be. It was just a bad day, don't be worried. I promise, I just need to get a good night of sleep and I'll be my normal self."

"Are you sure?" Wes asked.

"Yes, I promise."

"You can tell me what's going on, you know that, right?"

"Yeah, of course."

Wes was silent as he held her. They stood there as the rain increased in strength. Just as it seemed to fade away, it started pouring again. Finally, Delilah pulled away and sat down in the mud. Wes sat next to her, put an arm around one shoulder, and rested his head on the other. Delilah reached up to ruffle his soaked hair, and he caught her hand as she lowered it, holding it in his own.

Headlights appeared down the road. The two jumped up and waved them down. An old junker pulled up behind them and a college girl rolled down the window. Delilah went to talk to her.

"Hey, could you get us to Aspen, or as far southwest as you're going?" she asked.

"Sure, I can get you near Aspen, but pull the blanket out of my trunk and put it down on the back seat before you get in."

They did, and then crawled in, sighing in relief at the warm, dry interior.

"Just warning you, I have Mace accessible right now. And a hunting knife. Just in case you're criminals," the girl said.

"No worries.We're just trying to get to Sedona," Wes said.

"I'm just trying to get home to Nevada. I keep getting held up cause this dumb car keeps needing repairs." She hit the dashboard as she said it, to teach the car a lesson. "I'm Sandra, by the way."

"Delilah and Wes."

"So why are you guys going to Sedona?"

Delilah sighed. "Delivering a box my ex left me."

"Why?"

"She left instructions for me to do so."

Sandra shrugged. She messed with some dials.

"I can't get radio right now. Ugh, and the cassette player doesn't work. Yeah, I don't even have a CD player. Ugh." Sandra sped down the highway fifteen miles over the speed limit. "I hate night driving. And rain driving."

Delilah and Wes were too tired to keep up a conversation, and soon fell silent. Delilah leaned against the window and drifted off a few times, but was always snapped back to consciousness by a sharp curve or bump. Wes didn't even try to sleep. He watched the mountains pass by in various hues of black and gray, watched bits of trees illuminated by headlights disappear back into the night as they passed. Sandra didn't seem to be familiar with fatigue, and drove for hours without so much as a yawn. They arrived in Aspen with the sunrise, and were dropped off near the cheapest hotel they could find.

They checked in with the dead man's cash, intending to take the day off and spend the night in Aspen.

"Alright, nonsmoking... two queens or one king?" the clerk asked.

Wes and Delilah looked at each other.

"One king?" Delilah said uncertainly.

"Yeah," said Wes.

They headed to their room and unloaded their stuff. Delilah changed into a long t-shirt with exercise shorts and flopped into the bed.

"I'm going to shower," Wes said.

"Alright."

He deliberated by the bathroom door for a minute.

"Do... you want to come?" he asked.

"Heh, you said cum," Delilah said.

"No, stop," he laughed and shook his head at her, "Seriously."

Delilah paused and tilted her head to the side thirty-two degrees after looking closely at him. "Okay. Sure."

She rolled off the bed and walked past Wes into the bathroom. She looked over her shoulder.

"Well, come on in," she said.

He did, and shut the door behind her.

"Okay," she said.

"Okay," he said.

"You know I haven't shaved in like, two weeks, right? Like, a while before we even started this trip," Delilah said.

"It's fine."

"Okay, just warning you."

She pulled her shirt and sports bra off, then her joggers and underwear. She was lean and fit, shoulders streamlining into a subtle "v" at the waist with barely visible abs, then curving out to her hips and down again through her legs.

"Nice," Wes said.

"Nice?" she laughed.

"Well... I mean..."

"I know. I'm hot. Hot as hell. You could literally fry an egg on my body," she said, smiling. "Okay, your turn."

"Now I feel insecure."

"No need. You're hot too, and exactly my type. Come on, weren't you a slut at some point?"

"Not with girls like you," he said, taking off his shirt to reveal a similar body, thin but with lean muscle.

"See, you have a very nice torso," Delilah said.

He took his pants and underwear off.

"And a nice dick. What do you have to be afraid of?" she continued.

"How are you so confident and comfortable?" Wes asked.

"Because nudity is nothing to me. I mean I value this type of nudity, because it represents something and it represents a point in a relationship, but tits and asses on their own really aren't... I mean, I would have no problem being a nudist. In all honesty, I believe clothes are overrated."

"I agree, but I'm just not good at all at putting that into practice," he laughed.

"It takes getting used to, because we've so often been told nudity is a *really* big deal, but I've normalized it for myself, if that makes sense."

"Huh. Yeah."

"You know what would be awful though?" Delilah asked, stepping into the shower.

"What?"

"Nudist C-Span. I would really hate that." They both laughed.

"You know I went to the gym a lot in high school, and that's also a place where nudity would bother me. Because of sharing all the equipment. You know?" He joined her in the shower and her eyes ran down his body as he did. He caught her looking and smirked at her. She raised her eyebrows and bit her lip before responding.

"That does bring up an interesting point, because STD's could be a problem if nudism became the social norm." As she said it, she stretched her arms behind him to adjust the stream of the shower, brushing against him as she did and running a hand down his arm as she moved away again. He placed a hand on her waist and she stepped closer to him, holding a hand on top of his and sliding it over her ribs to the small of her back. He used his other hand to brush water laden locks of hair out of her face and continued the discussion of nudism, which lasted the duration of the shower, as did the light movement of hands over wet skin. When they got out they were debating what uniforms would have to remain.

"I'm just saying, I'd want a waiter to be wearing underwear at least, because there's a lot of crotch level food in a restaurant kitchen," Delilah said.

"Is there?"

"Yeah, I've waited in a lot of restaurants, I would know."

"I don't think that means they need clothes though. Cops would still need their gear, and construction workers, they'd need clothing for safety reasons, but with waiters it's just the social taboo of the crotch area that creates the issue," Wes said.

"It's *not* just a taboo, pee comes from that region, and a shit load of bacteria."

"That's fair." Wes fell into bed and patted the space next to him.

Delilah crawled in and laid down, just brushing up against him. They turned their heads in towards each other. Wes leaned in and pecked her lips. Delilah caught the back of his head and pulled him in again, turning their kiss into something that made their muscles clench and raised goosebumps on their skin. Delilah nuzzled her mouth into his neck, but he pulled back when she tried to give him a hickey.

"No, I hate hickeys, they're painful."

"Aww, I'm sorry. I forget other people don't like pain."

"You're into that stuff?"

"Oh yeah."

"So," he smiles, "Things... like this?"

He pinned her arms above her head to kiss her neck, and she laughed in surprise.

"*Yes* actually, that's hot as hell," Delilah said.

Wes giggled against her neck and it sent chills down her back. She tucked her face between his head and shoulder and smiled at the smell of his hair. Finally they broke apart and rolled into their own sides of the bed.

"You're good at that. And I don't say that very often because it's pretty hard to turn me on," Delilah said.

"Oh, you have no idea."

"Don't I?"

"You wanna go again?"

"Come at me," Delilah said, in a sarcastically challenging voice.

"Oh, you wanna go?" Wes mimicked her tone.

"Yeah, but I better not. Because then we'll have sex."

"Okay, so...."

"We're not going to... well-- no, better not. Distract me."

"Sure..." he thought for a moment, "You know, you never really said what your worst fear was,"

"Yeah I did. Cockroaches."

"Bullshit."

"You really want to know my worst fear?"

"Yeah."

"Fine. Okay, yeah, fine, I'll tell you. Inadequacy. Disappointing my mother and father, letting down my family, not being the best, not making a mark, not being *good enough.* I don't know what for. Just in general. I have nightmares about my mom yelling at me for getting a C and me trying to respond but I can't. I have dreams about how much of a failure I am, because *I AM,* I am *nothing,* Wes. I've accomplished... *nothing,*" she said, frustration dissolving into despair as she finished.

"But look at how amazing you've become. Have you ever really evaluated *yourself,* instead of your belongings and accomplishments? I've known you... a while actually, ever since I first sold you two grams of weed. Between the diner, drugs, and random meet ups I guess I spent a lot of time with you, but honestly... it was never enough. Even spending my entire day with you, I want to be closer to you all the time, I want to know you're next to me when I sleep and I want to see you in my dreams. Delilah... I --"

"Don't. Don't say it," she snapped.

"What do you mean? Why not?" Wes looked at her in alarm.

"Because I don't want to hear it, and I'm not going to say it back. Please, Wes, just... don't say it." Delilah said it harshly, but her eyes were soft with anxiety.

Wes shook his head a bit. He ran his hand through his hair.

"I don't understand," he murmured.

"Good," she snapped.

"I really wish I understood."

"Do you?"

"You won't even let me say it?" he asked.

"NO."

"I thought we were doing really well, especially just now."

Delilah took a long inhale, then exhale. "I'm sorry. Don't take my lack of expression as lack of emotion. I just... right now... I don't feel like I can exchange those kinds of thoughts, but that doesn't mean I don't have them."

Delilah's feelings mirrored his almost perfectly. When she kissed him she felt fire in her veins and tasted promise on his lips. When she looked into his eyes she saw his entire mind sprawled out, all for her exploration. When he wrapped around her she felt safe.

"Yeah, fine. I don't get it. But okay," he said.

"Really. I'm sorry."

"Don't be. It's okay." Wes leaned in to kiss her on the forehead and wrapped an arm around her shoulder, "But the way you're talking...."

"Wes... I'm okay, just because I talk shit about myself doesn't mean I actually feel that way."

He takes a deep breath and then rolls his lips against each other, "It makes me nervous, I don't know if you really are okay."

"I *am*. I promise."

"If you're sure."

"I am. Well, what are we going to do today?" Delilah asked, changing the subject.

"Nap, since we didn't really sleep last night, watch crap TV, and order a pizza with whatever money we have left?" Wes asked.

"Yes, please." Delilah called the front desk and asked for the number of the nearest, cheapest pizza place while Wes channel surfed to find a show about weddings, home renovations, or weight loss.

Delilah wrote the number down, thanked the clerk, and hung up.

"So, we have eighteen dollars left. What can that get us?" Delilah asked.

"We can definitely afford a large. Pepperoni?"

"Sure." Delilah placed the order and leaned back to watch brides get harassed by their family members over wedding decisions.

After an episode, the pizza arrived, and Delilah answered the door wrapped in a sheet. She gave the delivery boy a decent tip and took the pizza back to the bed.

"Are you okay with eating on the bed?" she asked.

"Yeah."

They laid out on the bedspread with the open box of pizza on their laps and watched a series of shows on TV. First, a mother of a bride insisted on wearing white to her daughter's wedding, then a seven hundred pound woman lost five hundred pounds, then the life of an unusually tall person (whose life was perfectly normal, except the person was tall). They made fun of the trash TV, and finished off the pizza. Delilah fell asleep on Wes's shoulder, then later he fell asleep on hers. They both tried to ignore mosquito bites, but failed every time the sheets brushed against one.

"I want to sleep but I don't feel like it," Delilah said later, looking across the bed at Wes.

"Same."

"Do you want to go out for a walk?" she asked.

"I don't want to get dressed."

"True."

"Have you ever seen *Pulp Fiction*?" Delilah asked.

"No."

"It's my favorite movie. I have the first fifteen minutes memorized."

"Let's hear it."

"Okay, so it opens up in a restaurant, with a couple sitting at a table across from each other, they're sort of grungy...." Delilah went on, and Wes listened to all the different inflections in her voice and watched all the movements of her lips.

He shifted positions while she talked about Europe, and drifted off while she was talking about foot massages. She slowly tapered her voice off until she became silent, and then she too drifted off to sleep.

The next morning it took them almost until noon just to get out of bed and get going. It was hard to keep going on and on, but it was even harder to go and then stop, and then get going again. Once they were on the road, however, they easily settled back into their routine. The views while they walked were deep, gorgeous, heavy and sweet like ganache.

That afternoon, as they walked down the road just outside of Aspen, Delilah noticed a minivan being driven and occupied predominantly by teenage boys. Without time to hesitate she pulled up her shirt and, sure enough, the van pulled over.

"Delilah, no!" Wes laughed.

She jogged to the driver's window. "We're trying to get to Sedona, but we'd love it if you could just take us Montrose. Farther if you can."

"I'd offer to take you even farther but we're picking friends up in Delta, and you'll have to sit on the floor as it is. Montrose works well, though," the lifeguard stereotype driver said.

"That's fine, thanks," said Delilah.

The sliding doors opened and Wes and Delilah climbed inside and found space on the floor.

"We're road-tripping to Vegas," the driver said.

The five other boys and two girls in the car whooped.

"What about you guys?" one of the girls asked.

"My ex left me a box with directions to deliver it to Sedona," Delilah said.

"That's weird."

"Yeah."

Delilah soon became irritated and drained being in a van full of teenagers on their way to Las Vegas. They still had three hours to Montrose.

"I brought cards!" someone shouted, pulling out a deck. "Who wants to play poker?"

"In the car?"

"Sure."

In the end, Wes and Delilah sat with their hands spread out to form a table while the other passengers gambled their spare change. Every once in awhile someone would say something stupid and Wes and Delilah twitched their eyebrows at each other and smiled almost imperceptibly.

"We can be the table this next round so you guys can play." Two people offered, but Wes and Delilah declined, saying they weren't that into poker, so they didn't mind just watching everyone else.

They sat there, across from each other, speaking silently in the middle of youth's torrential energy.


As they drove towards Montrose, the teens continued talking to each other, without paying Wes and Delilah any attention.

"Where do you want to be dropped off?" asked the driver.

"I don't know, anywhere," Delilah said.

"Alright." He drove them near the south side of town and dropped them off.

They all waved to each other, and then the group was off towards their glamourous Vegas adventure. Wes and Delilah were three hours closer to Sedona.

"Well," said Wes.

"Time to head that way," Delilah checked the position of the sun and then pointed southwest.

"Man...."

"I know, I'm getting tired of it too. But it's like you said, you just have to push through it until it becomes fun again," Delilah said.

"I just want to get to Sedona and open that box."

"Yeah, I know. But right now, we just have to keep walking, and hope someone pulls over for us."

They headed off down the road.

"Do you want me to entertain you with my vast collection of jokes?" Wes asked.

"Oh no. Fine, go ahead."

"Okay. What do you call a judgmental prisoner going down the stairs?"

Delilah sighed, "A condescending con descending."

"Oo, very good!"

That went on for a half hour or so, but it got boring after that.

"Want to play a riddle game?" Delilah asked.

"How's it work?"

"You have to figure it out. Okay, if A is the road and B is that telephone wire, C is that tree. Now you try; if A is that tree and B is that cloud, what is C?"

155

"Umm... the road?"

"No, C is my shirt. Alright...."

Delilah knew enough road games to keep them occupied for a couple of hours. They took turns holding their thumbs out, but no one offered them a ride.

"*Someone take us to Prescott so we can drop of this weed and get to Sedona so we can find out WHAT THE HELL is in that GODDAMN BOX!*" Delilah shouted.

"I'm with you, but maybe don't shout about drug drop offs."

"No one can hear us. They're all in their cars. But I see your point. So, even if Sedona is closer, should we still go to Prescott first?"

"I'd say so. I want to get this drop off done," Wes said.

"Okay, good plan."

Delilah started humming, and then she and Wes sang together for a while. A sedan pulled over.

"Oh, thank heavens," Delilah said.

"Where are you headed?" the man driving called out.

"Prescott, Arizona, or anywhere on the way," Wes called back.

They walked up to the car.

"Sorry, I'm actually turning north in about twenty miles. But I can take you that far," he said.

"Well, we'd appreciate that," Delilah said.

Twenty minutes later they were back on the road. This time a truck pulled over almost immediately. A tanned woman, looking like the type of person who would take nudes wrapped in the American flag, stepped out to talk to them. She was in cowboy boots and cut off jean shorts.

"We're trying to get to Prescott," Delilah said.

"Well, aren't you in luck! I'm on my way to Red Mesa. That will get you in the right state, even if it's only the edge," she said.

"You can actually take us to Arizona?" Wes asked.

"She can take us to Arizona!" Delilah said in excitement and relief.

"WE'VE GOT A RIDE TO ARIZONA!" Wes and Delilah hugged and jumped up and down.

"What, have you had a tough time getting picked up?" the woman asked.

"We just haven't been making great time," Delilah explained, releasing Wes.

"Good thing I stopped then. One of you is going to have to squeeze in the mini seat behind the passenger seat."

"I can," Delilah offered, and they climbed in.

"It'll be about four hours and twenty minutes," said the driver.

"Four twenty, sounds good," Wes said, smirking back at Delilah.

"I'm Daphne."

"Wes and Delilah."

"So, what brings you to Arizona?" she asked.

Delilah sighed. "My ex-lover left me a box with directions to deliver it in person. And we're not allowed to open it."

"Fascinating," Daphne said.

"Yeah, fascinating," Delilah said.

"I love the southwest. Or anywhere in the south, really, but the southwest is *so* gorgeous, and so interesting!" Daphne went on, but Delilah found it hard to pay attention.

The sign welcoming drivers to Arizona came into view, and Wes and Delilah cheered.

"It's Arizona!" Delilah called.

"Woohoo! We're in the right state!"

"ARIZONA!" Delilah shouted.

"FUCK YEAH, ARIZONA!" Wes responded.

Daphne just smiled.

Red Mesa was relatively flat, except for the red mesa itself. The sky, pink from the setting sun and filled with cotton ball clouds, stretched farther than Delilah had ever been used to seeing. Dry shrubs stuck up from pale dirt. They stood outside Daphne's house, a very southwestern adobe home, with succulents lining the path to the front door, and smooth stones instead of grass for a lawn.

"You'll want to make sure all your water bottles are full before leaving town," Daphne said. "And I'll give you an extra gallon just in case. But I guess you need somewhere to spend the night first."

"Yeah," said Delilah.

"Well, I can put some sleeping bags in the garage for you. Just remember, gun laws are lax here so you better not mess with me or my stuff."

"We won't. Thank you so much," Wes said.

They headed inside, which was covered in Native American rugs and artwork, metal lizards and kokopellis playing flutes. They sat in the kitchen while Daphne got sleeping pads and bags for the garage. They settled in, set their stuff down, and stripped down for bed. They both snuggled into their sleeping bags, washed with lavender scented detergent and carefully laid out, perfectly smooth.

The next morning Daphne made them oatmeal and offered them her shower. They ate and then decided showering *could* wait, but probably shouldn't. They showered, and were glad they did, because they really did feel better afterwards, their cleaner bodies allowing clearer minds.

"Wes," Delilah said.

"Yeah?"

"How long do you think it will be until we get to Prescott?"

"I don't know."

"I want to know," she said.

"I can't help with that."

"Wes."

"What?"

"Have you ever hot boxed a dumpster?" she asked.

"What?"

"Smoked a bunch of weed in a dumpster, but with the top on so it fills with the smoke, so every time you breath in it's just like... dude."

"No, I know what hot boxing is I've just never done it in a dumpster."

"I have. It was actually fun. But really stupid."

"Why do you bring it up?" Wes asked.

"I don't know, I just sort of thought of that."

Wes laughed, "Okay."

"We should get going." Delilah headed out. Wes tilted his head in confusion, and then he followed her.

The landscape, though gorgeous, was unwelcoming to those who weren't used to it. Wes and Delilah found the sun too aggressive, and the dust bothersome. Wes shielded his eyes and looked to the horizon. There were plenty of cars passing them, but none seemed interested in picking them up.

"You know," Wes said, "if this were the fifties, we'd be having no problem at all."

"Yeah, but would you really want to live in the fifties?"

"No."

"Yeah, me neither. Can you imagine? I'd be crucified," Delilah said.

"You are certainly not fifties material."

"Thank heavens."

Wes waved with increased vigor at the next car, but was ignored.

"Should I take my shirt off again?" Delilah asked, laughing.

"*No*... I mean, maybe. You know what, no," said Wes.

"I'm ready to jump out in front of one of these cars in order to get a ride right now. You know what this feels like? It feels like this one time when I waited eleven hours to see Collecting Matches. It was amazing because I was front row. I waited eleven hours just to get into the venue, and when I did there was only half an hour left before they came on. Even though I'd easily withstood the eleven hours, those thirty minutes felt *so long.* If we hadn't started playing cards with the people next to us, it would have been pure hell."

"That's something I'd like to do. Go to some concert I'm super passionate about."

"Well, someday you'll get a chance," Delilah said.

A pickup truck with "Jesus King" spray painted across it, as well as other odd phrases that didn't quite make sense, such as "A Bible is An Application For Heaven!" pulled up behind them, and they turned to talk to the driver.

"Where are you two headed?" the driver, an older, sun-worn man, asked.

"Prescott!" Delilah called.

"Any place specific?"

"Wes, could you get the address out of my pack?"

Wes quickly unzipped her pack and got the slip with the address out of the tampon box, ran back to the driver, and handed it to him.

"I can take you here," he said.

"Really?" Delilah asked, ecstatically.

"Sure."

Wes and Delilah's eyes met and they beamed.

"Thank you *so* much!" Wes said.

"Really, thank you!" Delilah said.

"Don't mention it. I just hope you're okay with riding in the bed, and you should probably lay down so we don't get pulled over. Also, take these, they're on me." He held out two worn Bibles and Wes took them with a nod.

"Thanks again," Wes said, and they both hopped into the bed, slinging their packs in first, and laid on their backs next to each other.

"What a nice guy!" Delilah said.

"Very Christian," Wes said, lifting the Bibles.

"You bet. Although to be honest I don't want to carry those around. We should probably just leave those here."

"I'm fine with that. Delilah, we're getting dropped off exactly where we need to be in Prescott, and we'll get there tonight."

"Wes! Wes, I can't believe it, we're getting to Prescott and then it's just, what, an hour to Sedona? Give or take? We're finally going to figure out *what's in this box!*"

"I know. I can't wait!"

"Imagine though, if we drop it off and the girl is just like, 'thanks' and doesn't even tell us what it is," Delilah said.

"We won't accept that. We're going to insist on figuring this out."

"Okay, I agree."

They laid there, watching the clouds shift in the pale blue sky which took on a golden hue as the afternoon progressed to evening, and Delilah reached over and slid her fingers through Wes's. He gave her hand a squeeze, and used the other to move her hair out of his face. The time, unexpectedly, slipped by easily, and their oddly blissful haven soon drew to a close as the Jesus King truck pulled into the driveway of a house that, though upper-class, was in great need of maintenance. They hopped out, waved goodbye to the man, and ran to the door. Wes dug the tampon box out of Delilah's pack and handed it to her, then knocked.

"Hey?" said the man who answered.

"Hi. We've got a delivery from Heritage Farms?" Delilah said.

"Ah, yes," he turned behind him to shout into the house, "GUYS! The weed is here, Meadow's stuff! Come on in, you two."

"Oh, we're just delivering --" Wes began but the man cut him off.

"Please, you came all this way, and any friend of Meadow's is a friend of mine. Come in and have some fun. I'm Joseph, by the way."

"Well, Joseph, I don't really feel like partying..." Delilah said.

"Then sit back and watch us act stupid. You'll have a blast. Please, I insist." He opened the door wider and gestured them inside.

"Well... fine." Delilah headed in and Wes followed.

They were met with cheers. A group of maybe ten people were sitting around a table with a bong and a few cases of beer.

"We're almost out. It's good you came!" one shouted.

Delilah pulled the bag out of the box and again, the group erupted in cheers and applause. Delilah smiled, but didn't mean it. She wasn't sure why she even came in. She didn't want to be around this right now.

"Make yourself comfortable. Cassie, move out of the way." Joseph made the group clear a spot for them on a couch, so they sat.

Wes and Delilah didn't do much from then on, besides laugh as their hosts slowly became incapacitated. Wes enjoyed himself anyway. Delilah just sat quietly. After an hour, a preteen appeared in the doorway to the living room.

"Go do your homework Kylie," Joseph said as he saw her.

"I already did. And I'm hungry."

"Dad's with his friends right now. Go to your room."

"I know you're stoned, Dad."

"Where'd you learn about that?"

"I'm in middle school. I know about getting high."

"Sweetheart, I'm not stoned. It's adult time right now, go... do your homework."

"You're such a wreck," Kylie said in scorn, turning to leave.

"HEY!" Joseph almost got up, but decided it wasn't worth it.

"Can I go talk to her?" Delilah asked, speaking for the first time since she'd arrived.

"Why?" Joseph asked.

"I don't know," Delilah said, honestly.

"Knock yourself out."

Delilah rose, but gestured for Wes to stay where he was. She walked down the hallway until she found a door emitting a soft light through the gaps around and underneath it. She knocked lightly.

"What do you want?" Kylie asked from inside.

"It's one of your dad's friends. Can we talk?" Delilah asked.

There was the sound of soft footsteps, then the door opened slightly.

"Why?" she asked.

"I feel like talking to someone sober," Delilah said.

Kylie looked her up and down, then opened the door wider for her.

"Thanks." Delilah walked in and sat on a beanbag, while Kylie sat on another one.

Kylie scoffed as she looked at Delilah's grungy, denim dominated shirt and shorts.

"Hey, the nineties called --" Kylie started.

"-- your mom just saw your face for the first time and regretted not getting an abortion."

"Holy shit."

"Don't mess with people this much older than you. And watch your language," Delilah said.

The walls of the room were covered in posters from metal bands, predominantly one with a thin, incredibly attractive lead singer. All of his posters were fairly cheesy; one was of him surrounded in flames, the other was of some metal monster with the band name across the top. Nothing too creative.

"You're into metal?" Delilah asked.

"Yeah. I don't like any of that pop crap," Kylie said.

"Don't knock anyone's music. You're not special just because you don't fawn over boy bands, alright?"

"I didn't say I was, gosh."

"But I bet you were thinking it."

Kylie didn't respond.

"I like metal too. I haven't really listened to it lately. I haven't listened to anything lately, it sucks. Do you like Collecting Matches?"

She shook her head. "I haven't really heard any of their work."

"What do you play music on?" Delilah asked.

Kylie went and got her phone and speaker and found Collecting Matches albums online. She pressed shuffle.

"NO, you can't put the albums on shuffle because the songs were very intentionally placed in that order. They're meant to be listened to as a whole." Delilah grabbed the phone and played "Forestry" off shuffle. "See, this is a really underrated album. I used to think I didn't like it as much as the others, but trust me, once you really listen to it a few times you'll grow to love it just as much as every other album. Possibly even more."

"Ah, I have heard this song. I don't know, I can't get into these guys."

"Well, I'm playing them anyway. You just have to listen to them a few times. You'll start to appreciate them. So, what's up with you?"

Kylie shrugged.

"The end of the school year must be coming up," Delilah prodded.

"Yeah. Finally."

"You don't like school."

"It's stupid, and it's a waste of time. I don't even learn anything. The only stuff I don't know is random crap I forget by next year," Kylie said.

"I felt the same way. I know it sucks but it's important. You really should try. I didn't, and now I wish I had."

"I still get all A's."

"Yeah, well you're in middle school. You actually have to do stuff in high school."

"We do stuff in middle school."

"You're going to do a lot more in high school. You might have to try," Delilah said.

Kylie pouted. "I'll probably drop out. Lots of successful people are drop outs."

"Yeah, well, first of all, a lot of them dropped out of ivy leagues, not high school. Most of them also had million dollar ideas. And they were geniuses. So tell me honestly. Are you a genius Kylie? Really?"

Kylie looked down. "No."

"Then stay in school."

"Who are you to be giving advice? You're hanging out with my dad."

"I know what not to do. I know what I should have done."

Kylie was saying something, but suddenly Delilah had stopped listening. She noticed, on Kylie's desk, a safety pin, and her mind immediately went to a different place.

The safety pin held memories for her, and the memories held pent up emotions. She realized she hadn't been well recently. The tentative bridge that held up the illusion of a stable reality shattered inside her. And, like a plastic knife being twisted into someone's torso, the shards immersed themselves in her being, turning into something that couldn't be removed without serious intervention. She knew that those who had never experienced it would never understand the difficult feeling, but it was this feeling that led her to realize she'd been slowly sinking through a layer of ice, and was just now falling into the dangerous depths below.

"Where's your bathroom?" Delilah asked.

"At the end of the hall," Kylie said.

"Thanks." Delilah walked down the hall and locked herself into the bathroom.

The room was small and cramped; there was a shower, toilet, and sink, all pushed up against each other, with just enough room to access each appliance. Delilah looked into the mirror above the sink and thought she looked different. Aged, maybe. Maybe she just looked cold. She closed her eyes and breathed in and out and tried to think her way back to safety, but that wasn't how this worked. Thinking with more concentration in her situation was about as useful as breathing more deeply into diseased lungs. And then she stopped thinking altogether. She checked the drawers under the sink and found a four-pack of razors. She took one out and snapped the end off the handle, then grabbed a nail clipper and cut the guard around the razor, exposing one corner. She didn't believe she would actually follow through, not after she had escaped it for so long. But in the end, she cut herself. Five times across her ankle. Each one burned as she did it, and the feeling lingered just a little bit once it was done. Then she noticed a pack of matches. She thought it must be some cruel trap for those to just appear in a bathroom, but despite this, in one fluid movement, she lit one, shook it out, and held the end into her skin, pulling it back at first, but then driving it back down with force. She didn't understand the relief that came with the sharp pain, but she enjoyed it. A pale, wrinkly section of skin appeared and she picked it off so it wouldn't blister, leaving behind a shimmering, pink circle. She did this two more times, pushing the match straight down without pulling it back at all, and larger pale circles appeared in her skin.

"Fuck," she said to her reflection. "I mean, really. Fuck. God dammit. What the fuck."

She took a hair tie and pulled her hair away from her face before kneeling on the floor with a washcloth to wipe away the beads of blood that had appeared and were beginning to spill down onto her foot. The cuts were deep enough that if she put a finger on each side of one, it would open and close like a mouth. She was disgusted by herself, by what she determined to be weakness, and what she defined as failure. She sat on the floor, head in her hands, and didn't cry. There was a knock on the door.

"Delilah?" It was Wes. "Are you okay?"

"I'm fine. I just feel sick," she called back.

"You're sure you're okay?"

"Yeah."

"Are you lying?"

"No."

"Would you tell me if you were?"

"Yes."

"...Can I come in?"

"No."

"Please?"

"NO. I'm fine. Really."

"Delilah."

"I mean it, Wes."

"...Okay, then." But he didn't walk away from the door.

"Go away," said Delilah.

He sighed, and walked back to the living room. He sat by himself and couldn't help but remember his brother.

Delilah, there on the bathroom floor, figured she'd be fine in a week or so. That's usually how it went. With Sedona coming up, she thought she would probably be lifted up more quickly, though she worried about a crash afterwards. But she hoped she would be fine.

She walked back into the living room and found people were starting to pull blankets and pillows out onto the floor, and were falling asleep on the couch. Wes curled up in a recliner, and began to drift off. Delilah looked at him and felt a bit warmer at the sight of him, curled up there adorably. As she walked past she ruffled his hair and kissed him on the forehead. He craned his neck to look at her and smiled.

Everyone else passed out pretty quickly, but Delilah and a girl named Carrie, who resembled a wax figurine with bleached white hair, ended up sitting in the kitchen, unable to sleep.

"You know," Delilah said, "I'm sort of regretting turning down that weed earlier."

"Sorry, Joseph already put everything away. And there isn't any alcohol left," Carrie said.

"Nothing at all?"

Carrie turned and started rummaging through cabinets. She held up a bottle of Butterscotch Schnapps.

"Ugh. That shit is way too sweet and weird. It's just not right," Delilah said.

"You wanna get drunk, or not?"

"Don't you have anything else?"

"No."

"Fuck." She held out her hand for the bottle, and took a swig.

"See, not that bad," said Carrie.

"First sip, not awful, after that... ugh. The taste just builds up."

"You seem experienced."

"I've been drunk on everything my grandma used to keep in her kitchen. And I've gotten high with every high school lacrosse player and every creep who had drugs to spare," said Delilah.

"And what, you enjoyed that? Living your life that way?"

"Of course not."

"Then why?"

"Because I was sad and alone, and I didn't have any other way to get away from reality for a while," Delilah said.

"You couldn't have read a book?"

"Psh. You have to put effort into reading. I did not have the energy to remove myself from my circumstances. And besides, reading just doesn't fuck around with neurotransmitters like alcohol does. I needed something easy and potent."

"And your solution was narcotics?" Carrie asked skeptically.

"You're one to judge."

"Yeah I know. I'm talking to myself as much as you," said Carrie.

"We're sad, aren't we?"

"A little bit. Sometimes." But she smiled. "That's alright with me."

"Look at all these losers, passed out at twelve thirty." Delilah laughed.

"To be fair, we stayed sober." Carrie took a swig of alcohol.

"About that...." Delilah held out her hand for the bottle.

By one o'clock they moved from the kitchen into Joseph's dark, dingy room, and were sitting on the bed playing, "would you rather."

By two o'clock they started "honesty hour" where they asked each other life questions and had to answer truthfully, and by two-thirty they'd stripped down to their underwear and bras, sitting cross-legged, though still fairly sober.

"I don't think there's enough of this left to really get wasted," Delilah said, holding up the last few swigs of liqueur.

"Yeah, there really wasn't much to begin with. I'm sort of buzzed though," Carrie said.

"I wish I had underwear like that," Delilah says, nodding to Carrie's robin's egg blue lace bra and dark red panties.

"It's definitely a confidence booster."

"Sometimes I also wish I had boobs," Delilah said.

"Sometimes I wish I was totally flat. Breasts are so fucking inconvenient. I have C's, and that's not even huge or anything, but they get in the way *so much*."

"I know, that's why I'm glad I'm an A-cup," Delilah said.

"And small, perky boobs are hot. I would probably fuck you, if you were gay," Carrie said.

"I'm bi, but I'm not into casual sex."

"Well, darn."

"But, if I were, I'd be down for that. You've got a really nice body," Delilah said.

"I'm fat."

"Not unhealthfully so. It looks good on you."

"Thanks. Really, I'm tired of people going, 'oh, honey, you're not chubby you're skinny', like we both know that's not true. Stop lying."

"Yeah." Delilah finished off the last sickeningly sweet swig of butterscotch schnapps and tossed the bottle on the floor, where it joined a pile of other empty bottles.

"Delilah, kiss me," Carrie said.

Delilah leaned over and kissed Carrie.

"Thanks," she said.

They both dropped down onto the bed and laid there.

By four o'clock they had both fallen asleep, sprawled out over the mess of blankets, limbs overlapping. They woke up five hours later.

"Are you leaving?" Carrie asked.

"Yeah, Wes and I should really get to Sedona."

"I can drive you," she said.

"No, it's no problem for us. We'll get there."

"It's no problem for me. Let me take you. I was going to leave town today anyway."

"Are you sure?" Delilah asked.

"Positive. Get Wes and pack up all your stuff. I can leave whenever."

"Well, alright." Delilah walked to the living room, which was dust colored from white light filtering through dark curtains, where Wes was still curled in a recliner. She shook his shoulder and he jerked awake.

"What?" he asked, groggily.

"I got us a ride to Sedona. We can be there in an hour," Delilah said.

"Really?"

She nodded. He yawned and scrambled out of the chair to get his pack. Carrie walked through the room and led them out to her car. It was a run-down two door, with little trunk space, parked on the curb. The morning was especially hot and the pavement was already giving off the smell of tar and asphalt. A lawnmower could be heard in the distance.

"I'm not sure if both your packs can fit in the trunk. You might want to throw one in the back." Carrie walked to the driver's door and unlocked the car. "I don't know why it's so hot this morning, it's not usually like this."

Wes put his pack in the trunk, and Delilah threw hers in the back and scooched in. Wes got into the front and Carrie got behind the wheel. She started the car and the morning radio program started to blare through the speakers.

"Oh, this show sucks," she said. "You can look through these CD's if you want."

Wes shuffled through them. "Delilah, any preference?"

"Does she have Collecting Matches?" Delilah asked.

"Yeah, she has a few albums."

"Choose one at random for me."

Wes picked out a red one and put it in.

"Hey, I love this," he said after half of the first song.

"Really?" Delilah asked.

"Yeah, it's great."

Delilah smiled. "I think so too."

"So, you guys have been hitchhiking all the way here from Iowa? Delilah, you told me all about it last night but I was sort of drunk and wasn't really paying attention," Carrie said.

"Yeah," Delilah said. "Yeah, my ex left me a box to deliver in Sedona and I don't know what's inside it."

"Wow. And you'll find out today maybe," Carrie said.

Delilah felt a bit faint after that statement. "Yeah. We're really getting close."

Carrie squealed with excitement for them. "That's so great you guys! You're going to have to text me about the contents, 'cause I'm dying to know."

"Will do. What's your number?"

Only an hour later Carrie dropped them off at the edge of Sedona, and then she was on her way. Wes and Delilah were alone again. They walked farther into town, ready to ask someone for directions to Amelia's. As they approached denser housing, Delilah stopped.

They stood at the edge of the road, overshadowed by the auburn and ochre stone structures that dominated the skyline. The crevices of their shoes, their knees, their clothes, filled with red dust. Delilah clutched a water bottle in her hands, and her expression sank into fear. Wes looked over at her.

"Hey, are you okay?" he asked.

"Yeah," she said, "yeah, but you know, I just... I don't know what's going to happen when I'm not trying to do this anymore. You know, when we're done."

He was silent. She looked down and drew the ball of her foot over the same section of dirt a few times, flattening it.

"I mean, I've been fine recently, mostly," she said "but I've been so focused on getting here to Sedona, that I haven't even thought about myself, or Lottie, or any of my responsibilities. And you've been so focused on it too, and on me, trying to help me get here. What if we finish this and we just crash? Because I'm not sure I'm able to keep myself up for more than a few months at a time. And I can't afford to treat any mental health problems, and you can't either, and...."

"We'll be fine after this. We'll find some other purpose, and get some cheap counseling or some kind of help. I mean, I'm sure there are options. Right?"

"I don't know. I dunno, Wes, I *don't know* what I'm supposed to do."

"Well. We'll ask someone in Sedona. We'll find the answers. Come on, let's go."

"I just feel lost," she said.

"I know. And I know you've lost someone, too, and that's hard."

But Delilah had felt the heartache of losing someone long before she had lost Lottie. It wasn't the loss of a person. It was just a loss that invaded her, and then lingered. It was similar to the homesickness she felt when she was alone in her room.

"Okay, let's go." Delilah walked forward, and Wes followed.

They started seeing more people, but no one could give them directions when they asked.

"This place better exist," Delilah said.

"It does, don't worry." Wes waved at someone on the corner and they jogged up to him.

"Hey, do you know where this street is?" Delilah asked, holding out the box.

"Well, that's not a street. It's a hiking trail. It goes through the desert," he said.

"Really?"

"Yeah, but, uh, I can tell you how to get there."

"That'd be great," said Wes.

"Alright then...." The man pulled out his phone to show them a route, and Wes wrote it down on his hand.

"Thanks so much," Delilah said, and they headed off.

"A trail," Wes said.

"Maybe she lives in a tent?"

"I guess so. Maybe she's a park ranger."

"It's possible," Delilah said. "I guess we'll just go around looking for someone named Amelia."

"Amelia R."

"Amelia R," Delilah sighed.

The trail wasn't too far, and they got there in under an hour. It was an understated trail. A simple sign stated it's existence, and there weren't many other trails around it. It stretched through dry bushes and hosts of small green lizards, leading away from the city and towards the arches and plateaus in the distance.

"Do you think it's her?" Delilah asked.

"It's gotta be," Wes said as they looked out to the trailer.

Delilah picked up into a jog, box in hand, towards the trailer. Her feet stirred up rusty dust and scared lizards back into the stiff bushes, and caused a sleeping cat to jolt awake and stretch into a standing position. The sun bounced on her curls and small pebbles embedded themselves in the soles of her sandals. Delilah arrived at the door and knocked. The door was simple metal, but it had a frosted glass window in the center. She waited, and then heard rustling inside. The door opened, and inside was a woman, looking like a goddess of the seventies in gentle bell-bottomed pants and a tie-dyed crop top. Her long dark hair was beginning to gray prematurely and fell almost to her waist. She had a sun worn face crinkling with confusion at the sight of her guests.

"I wasn't expecting anyone," she said.

"We have a delivery. From Lottie Druring, you're Amelia right?" Delilah asked.

"Yeah, yeah, I'm Amelia...Really? Lottie? I didn't think she was sending me anything... Come on in." Amelia held the door open as they entered, then offered them a seat on her bed.

"So..." Delilah said as she sat down, not really sure how to begin. "Lottie's dead. She killed herself."

Amelia's mouth sank open, and she was silent for a while. "Oh. Oh.... I see."

"She left this for me to deliver to you."

"Oh." Amelia looked down at her sheets on the bed.

"I'm sorry. Were you close?" Delilah asked.

"A while ago. A while ago she visited me on and off, a week or so each time, once longer. She told her family a few lies... she thought about staying, but it was too hot and she didn't appreciate the lifestyle I live. I don't blame her." She sat up on her knees to get a polaroid off the wall and handed it to them.

It showed Lottie looking over the edge of some red cliff down at the camera and smiling. She was framed by a pure blue sky above, and light red stone below.

"Did you guys come out from Iowa?" Amelia asked, keeping her grief pent up for later.

"We went to Iowa from Michigan by train, and then hitchhiked here," Wes said as Delilah stared down at the polaroid.

"Then you're probably wondering what's in this box," she said. She walked to a cabinet and pulled out a box cutter and started slicing through twine, tape, and paper until the box opened.

Inside was a plastic gallon bag filled with small white pills. The bag read "Xanax."

"So it was drugs after all," Delilah said.

"How did she get all this?" Amelia asked.

"I don't know," Delilah said. "Maybe she managed to rob a few pharmacies. Or had someone else do it for her."

"Lottie had a way of getting what she wanted," Amelia said. "I'll get some cash for you guys."

"You're paying us?" Wes asked.

"Well I would hope so." Delilah said, looking at Wes. "We need to get home somehow."

"I have to pay someone for this. Besides, it's probably what she wanted." Amelia opened a pantry and pulled out a duffle bag full of cash.

"Here's twenty thousand a piece." She said, pulling out a few wads of cash.

"Hold up friend. If you're going to pay us, I expect a fair wage." Delilah said.

"It's forty thousand dollars."

"Xanax sells for one to five dollars a pill *at least*, and there are more than forty thousand pills in there, plus we went through *all* of this shit to get here, you have no idea, seriously. Besides, Lottie was in love with me. She sent me here to give me a second chance at life and that takes more than forty thousand," Delilah said.

"Oh, I'm sorry, what would you suggest?" Amelia's eyes drove into Delilah's, but Delilah didn't blink.

"A hundred thousand between the two of us," Delilah said.

Wes looked at her in surprise.

"You're not going to use the money anyway, judging by your living conditions. I mean, if you wanted materialistic joy you wouldn't be living in a trailer like this," Delilah said.

Amelia looked her up and down. "Well. I can't say you're wrong. Fine, take it, I don't give a shit."

"I appreciate that. So, is this what you do?"

"Casually, yes." She opened her cabinets to reveal bags and bottles of various prescription drugs. "I also write."

"Like Delilah said, you could afford a lot more than this trailer," Wes said.

"I could. But I don't want it. I'll probably dump most of it off at a charity sometime soon. But it might need to be laundered, I don't know. Delilah, go ahead and shove the pills in that cabinet somewhere." Amelia walked back to the bed, dropped ten stacks of money bound and labeled "10,000" in Wes's lap, and flopped down onto it while Delilah went and placed the bag between a few bottles of Serraquil.

"So why do you do it, if not for the money?"

She smiled faintly and shook her head before responding, "Well... gosh, I guess I like it. I like the people in it, though most of them are pissed at me now, cause... well... as you can imagine the authorities got involved. With them. Not me. I could have done more for all my people, but I didn't. Nothing at all, actually...."

"Well, I don't know the situation well enough to comment," Delilah said.

"I can't believe this," Amelia said. "I can't believe she's dead."

Wes and Delilah sat together as Amelia closed her eyes for a few moments. She opened them.

"I need some time to myself. But you guys are free to come back tomorrow if you want."

"Okay, of course." Delilah led the way out.

They walked outside, and once the trailer receded into the distance behind them, Delilah sat on a rock and stored the money away in her pack, keeping ten one hundred dollar bills in her bra for easy access.

"Wes," she said faintly.

"Delilah."

"A hundred thousand dollars, for a shoebox full of Xanax and a cross-country trip. It was drugs. The whole time."

"I know."

"She had me deliver it so I'd get a bunch of easy money," she said.

"Yeah."

"And now we have money."

"I think it's yours," Wes said.

"No. It's ours," she said.

Wes paused for several seconds. "You sure?"

"I'm sure," said Delilah. "It's over."

"It's over."

"I can't believe it," Delilah said.

Wes sat in the dirt next to her, putting his head at her knee level. A soft breeze caught their hair. He looked over and noticed her ankle, with five red stripes and three brownish circular patches bordered with pink. He brushed his fingers against it and Delilah jerked it away.

"Delilah...."

"Wes, it's fine!"

"No, it's not, when did this happen?" he asked.

"It doesn't matter. Wes, please, I have it under control, I don't want to talk about it." She didn't meet his eyes as she said it. He stared up at her profile, forehead curving into her nose, curving into her lips, over her chin, and down her throat. Her cheekbone sat, scarcely visible, in a smear towards her lips. Her jaw created a blended line between her neck and her face. The eye he watched was downturned, lashes falling over it, iris gleaming dark grey-blue.

"Please, Delilah. Tell me what I can do."

"You can't do anything," she snapped. "It's fine."

"It's not. It's really not. *You're* not."

"I'm feeling better now. I, I was just anxious and all pumped up in a negative way. I'm better now. Can we please just get into town, get a meal, find a hotel?"

Wes looked up at her and felt lost. "Yeah... sure." But he didn't want to drop it.

"I say we forget about responsibility, and what we're going to do next. Let's do some touring, then just go to a nice restaurant, have a fancy meal complete with appetizers and drinks and dessert, and then get a suite at some great hotel and just wind down and enjoy ourselves," said Delilah.

"Yeah, that sounds nice," said Wes, but the worry didn't leave his eyes.

They walked into town and got a ride to the downtown area, where they got directions to the most expensive hotel room in town. They got a room, and when they walked in the temperature had been set to seventy-three degrees Fahrenheit, and the smell of rosewater had been meticulously maintained. The sheets were made from bamboo, the mattress foam arranged in layers and shapes designed for luxury. All perfectly white, just like the carpet, the spotless bathtub, and the delicate vials of lotions and oatmeal soaps that unwrapped like candy bars. The chrome appliances gleamed. The flat screen television set was unnecessarily large.

"These are the softest sheets I've felt in my entire life," Delilah said.

Wes walked over to feel them and agreed.

They dropped their packs in the entry way, out of sight.

"So," said Wes. "Would you like to go shopping downtown?"

"That sounds fun." Delilah looped her fingers through his and they headed back into the heat, carrying light conversations between their smiling lips which burst into giggles as the stepped outside. The sidewalk was hot, brightened by the sun which shone a bit too close to the surface of the earth.

They walked through boutiques, and Delilah found a gorgeous light blue, high-low dress that complimented her complexion and flowed gracefully around her fine figure. Wes found a sharp, lightweight, blue suit, which gave him a new found authority.

They walked downtown and saw advertised helicopter rides for sale, and booked the next available flight, which was in just two hours. They paid someone to drive them out to the airfield and, after completing paperwork, were lifted off the ground. They went up over the wide red expanse of the earth, where they saw the red dust turn to green patches of forest and rivers which gleamed the color of Delilah's eyes. Wes noticed and mentioned it to her, and her lips twitched but didn't pull all the way into a smile. Then they were level with the stone structures, those asymmetrical ochre and rust towers.

Wes wrapped an arm around Delilah's shoulder and she leaned into his, and his free hand took hers as he touched his lips to her hair. Delilah, upon seeing all this land from above, felt the oddity in which she could sense herself, as well as Wes, from above. Her emotions swayed and quivered, and her eyes watered. Finally a tear fell just as they touched back to the ground, the blades of the helicopter stirring up a small dust storm. Wes didn't see Delilah's tear, and she was glad he didn't.

That night they walked into a restaurant where everything was pale wood and industrial metal, with corrugated steel walls and a network of air plants strung over the tables. Delilah was in her new dress, Wes in his new suit. Delilah looked radiant, eyes at attention and skin glowing, with just a slight flush. Wes assumed this meant she was feeling better, overlooking the anxiety behind it.

"What are you getting?" Wes asked.

"I don't know, something I'd normally disqualify automatically because of its price," Delilah said.

"I'd get steak, but I sort of want something more unique."

"Same."

"We could share one of the family platters."

"Yeah, that sounds good," said Delilah.

The waiter came for their drink orders.

"I'll have water and I think we'll get a bottle of..." She looked at the drink menu and picked a wine, "Merlot."

"Anything else?" he asked, looking to Wes.

"Just water, thanks."

The waiter walked off and Wes and Delilah turned back to the menu.

"Maybe something vegan," Wes said.

"Yeah, maybe."

Wes glanced up at her and scanned her expression. She looked up and met his eyes and smiled, but the smile was taught and isolated to her lips.

"You okay?" he asked.

"Yeah. I guess I'm sort of worn out. I'm very glad to be having dinner with you though." She smiled and leaned over the table to kiss him, stretching awkwardly and carefully keeping her dress away from the candles arranged in the center of the table.

"Alright," he said, but couldn't quite shake his feeling of unease.

"They have duck here. I haven't had duck before," Delilah said

"It's good. You should get it. And if you don't like it, we can send it back." He smiled at their wealth, and she mirrored the expression.


That night they got back to the hotel and laid together for a while, her head resting on his shoulder.

"Wes, I know it hasn't been long since dinner, but you know what I'm really craving?" Delilah asked.

"What?"

"Bagels. I'd really love a bagel right now. With some cream cheese," she said.

"Delilah, are you asking me to go pick up a bagel for you?"

"Might as well make it a dozen. And don't forget the cream cheese."

"Alright, fine, I'll do it for you"

"Thanks, babe," Delilah called after him as he left.

Wes found a bagel place and decided what assortment to get for Delilah. He chose a mix of whole wheat, blueberry, and cinnamon-sugar, with both plain and strawberry cream cheese.

That night, Amelia shuffled through her drugs. Didn't she have more Serraquil than that? She knew she did. She decided she should start weighing her stuff more often.

The night was not inky or velvety but clear, and cool. As Delilah sat in the room, breathing in air through the window she had opened, she immediately assumed it was what drowning must feel like. Because, clear as it was, she couldn't breathe. She closed her eyes and inhaled, but her lungs still felt empty and dry. Finally she left the window and went to the bed.

Delilah was alone, and she was lost in waves she couldn't see above. She saw the fully stocked minibar. In her pocket was the Serraquil. And she knew a combination of the two would be more than she needed.

She thought she heard the rain, but it was only the wind.

Wes came back with a bag full of bagels, which later repulsed him, and he saw her there, looking awful, worse than any human he had ever seen. There were two or three pills left on the sheets. Wes collapsed in on himself. He crumpled into the side of the bed and began to weep and panic. His body turned to static in his fear. He took her hand in his and used the other to stroke her face.

"What'd you do? Why, Delilah? No! I love you, I love you. *I love you!* What happened? Why did you do this?"

Delilah was higher than she could comprehend. "No, nobody loves me. Nobody fucking loves me, you *fucking* liar. Nobody. NOTHING, IT'S NOTHING, nobody....You fucking liar..."

"Delilah please, no. I love you. I love you so fucking much --"

"No, no one loves me. It doesn't matter, nothing does, nobody...."

*"SOMEBODY COME! HELP, SOMEBODY! PLEASE HELP! CALL 911! OH, GOD, OH, GOD! FOR FUCK'S SAKE, SOMEBODY HELP US!"* Wes turned from her briefly, ran and opened the door to scream out into the hallway. He ran back in an instant.

Delilah managed to grab his hand and squeeze it a little.

"I can't feel anything, I don't feel anything. I don't feel, not even for you...." But it was a lie.

"Delilah, Delilah!"

The world was spinning, the fog was encroaching and surrounding her. Everything was red like rust, like dust. The fine red powder enveloped her, swirling into her lungs and veins. It finally reached her heart, moved into her arteries. Her disease was finally winning.

She couldn't think.

She couldn't breathe.

She could hardly see.

Her mind spun, and she could feel the landscape of it. Her mind was all static and fog, her body escaping her, too heavy.

*I want to leave,* she thought. *Let me go. It's killing me.*

And Delilah had nothing holding her to the earth because she hadn't found a meaning for herself.

But then, for just long enough, she became lucid. She turned her head to look out the window, and the moon was almost full. Its light turned the red rock to deep black silhouettes, and she realized that what happened to her wasn't fair. A meaning gathered together in her mind and became a foothold. She could feel her emotions and their landscape, she could feel the crevices of her thoughts, and she realized she had something to fight for. Panic hit like lightning when she realized she had made a mistake.

Wes stared into her eyes, saw those two gun barrels, and told her, "I love you."

She look into his eyes and wanted to say it back, she wanted to say, "I'm so sorry, I love you, I love you so much. I made a mistake, the worst one of my life, and I don't really want to leave you."

She wanted to tell him to go and be happy, and forgive her, and don't dwell on her. She wanted him to know she loved him as much as he loved her, but she couldn't find her voice, and though her lips parted, they made no sound.

From that place she felt so much fear. Her body had become it. She just wanted to talk to her parents again. She wanted to hold Wes, but she was too weak to reach for him. Something loud and chaotic was happening around her. People were touching her and shouting, and someone was crying. The world faded out.

Wes sat in the hospital, not alone, not in some dark space with flickering lights but in the middle of a seating area where athletes with sprained ankles laughed to each other, and freshly stitched wounds were admired by their owners. It all took place among bright white tiles and carpet with vague patterns swirling through it. Wes sat with his head in hands, eyes closed, gasping for breath as he choked on his fear.

He *had* to believe in her. She was strong, she could fight, she would live. He prayed, despite his lack of faith, a common thing at times like these.

He prayed under his breath over and over, "*Let her live*, oh, God, *let her live,* bring her back to me, free her from her pain and bring her back to me."

He really believed in her.

She'd go to a hospital, but she'd get out. They'd use their money to buy some land and start a nursery for desert plants. He knew now, without a doubt, he'd marry her. He'd buy her a rose quartz ring and they'd run that nursery together, potting succulents and dotting dirt on each other's faces, exchanging words that burst into laughs. He'd wake up to Sedona sunrises turning her white hair to bright pink, her body covered in a plain white down comforter. Their house would be adobe, and filled with dreamcatchers and crystals and rugs, with beautiful dark wood floors that chilled their feet in the morning. And when she opened her eyes, the dark blue would be sky blue from the way the light reflected in them. Her lips would curve into a smile and then a yawn, and she'd stretch a long lean arm around the back of his neck, nuzzle her face into his chest before drifting off again. He would bury his face in her hair, inhaling its bright, heavy scent, and he too would drift off. They'd have breakfast together in a kitchen with an earth tone color scheme, plants lining the many window sills, morning light illuminating modest tile countertops and dark wood cabinets.

Maybe, someday, they'd have a little girl with dark curly hair, dark brown or possibly blue eyes, and pale skin. She'd grow to be lean like her parents, sharp like Delilah and sweet like Wes. She would smile wide and often, she'd be their joy. They'd stay together until his hair was as white as Delilah's, until their skin stretched away from their bones. All those years together, hiking the red trails and smelling the butterscotch bark of the Ponderosa Pine. All those sunrises that turn the high, wide sky gold, but reflect pink on the clouds, with storms gathered miles away, their lightning a daily spectacle all through July. The gold sky set against the red ridges, the rocks that rise and fall. That whole life they would have, it could make him cry with joy at the thought.

He really believed she would make it.

The doctor emerged from the double doors he wasn't allowed behind. Her face could not be read, she was entirely professional. She was in light green scrubs, straightened blonde hair pulled back, wearing running shoes that absorbed the sound of her footsteps. Wes stared intently at her as she approached, and stood once she came close. Delilah had to be okay, someone like her.

The doctor's lips tightened. "I'm sorry. She didn't make it."

Time froze as he closed his eyes and the noise around him was overpowered by the crackle of static in his head. He couldn't process it, he couldn't think about anything. And as soon as his mind began turning again, he couldn't feel his body, he was too occupied by the thought of hers. What did she look like without a blush in her cheeks, without the roll of muscles under skin? Was it even possible for her to lie lifeless, alone? He felt a sense of loss and a loss of purpose, but stronger than everything else was his building rage. At her mom, at her family, at anyone who didn't try to do something for her and that included himself, that included everyone they'd met together. He opened his eyes and realized the doctor was trying to talk to him but he stood up and walked to the bathroom, wanting to be alone, seeing nothing but the various shades of blue carpet beneath his feet as he stared at the floor. He pushed into the single stall bathroom and slammed the door shut behind him, locking it. He pushed the heels of his hands against his temples and paced across the bathroom, shaking his head and impulsively pulling a fist back and then slamming it forward into the white tile wall. He hit it hard enough for his bones to crunch and his knuckles to bleed but he didn't feel it and he didn't hear himself cry out. He sank to the floor and his body convulsed with sobs.

"God," he choked on the word, and hoped Delilah had been right on the subject. After all, she deserved something better than the life she got on earth, she was light gathered into flesh and she deserved a loving household, a circle of good friends and a promising future but what did she get? She was born into a chance at that bright future but her community wouldn't let her live it in peace, her brain refused to function in the way her mind deserved, and she ended up in that hospital, another young suicide victim.

He knew he had to gather himself. He had to give the hospital her information, he had to answer any questions they had for him. He was beginning to feel the pain in his hand. There were many things that needed to be taken care of. But that night, all he could do was stare at nothing, feeling everything, and when he finally stood to rest a hand on the doorknob, all he wanted was to open it and see her leaning against a pink tile countertop, mouth pulled into a smile as she went to get a pot of coffee.